Into the Ruins

Issue I

Spring 2016

Published 2016 by Figuration Press

Into the Ruins is a project and publication of Figuration Press,
a small publication house focused on alternate visions of the future
and alternate ways of understanding the world,
particularly in ecological contexts.

intotheruins.com

figurationpress.com

ISBN 10: 0692699163
ISBN 13: 978-0692699164

Issue 1
Spring 2016

TABLE OF CONTENTS

Preamble

Stories

Reviews

Coda

PREAMBLE

A FUTURE ON EARTH
BY JOEL CARIS

It's most a matter of expectations.

Each day that we awaken and reset our feet on this earth, the future spirals out in front of us in kaleidoscopic possibility. Those possibilities are influenced by a galaxy of factors, some of which are within our control and many more of which are not. Yet despite our limited control, I suspect most of us—and I know I myself—project our own expected future onto the world. We often come into the day pre-purposed, and even if we give that day over to the vagaries of human existence, we rarely will give our month, our year, our entire lives over to the same. Again and again, society tells us we're in control. While there's an important truth to that, there's a (probably more) important truth to the lack of control that our society ignores to our collective detriment.

We do not get to determine our future. Yes, we influence it every day with a multitude of decisions and there's no doubt that we can carry ourselves forward bright into the day, or drop dark into hiding, or more often muddle ourselves somewhere in between. We have a profound impact on the shape of our lives through the decisions we do and don't make. Yet the world is a very large and complex place made up of trillions of other living creatures, making their own decisions and conducting their own actions. Meanwhile, whirling around these uncountable actions and decisions are the natural processes that bend and shape, create and destroy our lives with every passing hour. That beautiful frenzy determines so much of the world we get to live in, and we have so very little influence over it.

This has never stopped me from projecting my expectations onto the future. I've done it my entire life, from imagining the work I would do, the places I would live, the people I would love, the way I would spend my days, the highs and lows I would experience. I could never begin to tally all the worlds I've crafted for myself—none of which have ever come to bear, except in perhaps the most passing of resemblance. It's the same way that, of the few people I've fallen in love with, none of them have ever resembled the person I imagined. Why? Aside from the obvious, it's because they are human beings, with all the astounding complexity and beauty that I am incapable of imagining to its realistic depth on my own. My mind cannot begin to match the creativity of a billions-year-old universe, or planet, or ecosystem—even if it's a product of all those.

Similarly, the actual future I live will never resemble to any true degree the futures I imagine. They are far too complex, creative, surprising, and dumbfounding for me to come up with them through contemplation alone. I challenge anyone reading this to tell me they saw the exact details of this presidential cycle coming; I don't think a single person could honestly claim to. And yet, I did read at least one speculative essay on fascism[1] years ago by a certain Archdruid that started to seem uncomfortably familiar as Donald Trump rose to prominence late last year. While I don't think that essay's predictions are yet fully coming to pass (who's looking forward to 2020?) it is a sharp reminder that, while we can never know the details of the future, that doesn't mean we can't unearth its potential shapes.

In other words, we can know, we just can't *know*. We can create facsimiles and imagine scenarios, but they will never be as rich as reality, and will never reflect it perfectly—particularly in its depth and texture. But that hardly means we're flying blind. In imagining the people we might fall in love with, we can fill in some of the details that likely will be accurate (though this may be a bad example, as there are perhaps few realms in which we are more consistently surprised than love). In imagining the future, we can take current realities and trends, and use that information to sketch out futures that may end up looking at least somewhat like the eventual, realized reality.

The problem is that our most common, collective visions of the future leave out the vast majority of relevant information. Most science fiction fixates on space travel (which is actually quite rare, and the downward trendlines of which are utterly ignored) and iPhones and other digital gadgets and, for the most part, discount everything else. When political, social, and economic trends are brought to bear upon the stories, they usually are forced into either a narrative of endless betterment (usually from a standard-issue American liberal perspective) or dystopian negative feedback loops. These elements, falsely and simplistically portrayed, also rarely have much of any impact on the technology of the setting, which still fits to the space travel and digital gadget trendlines and most often varies only in whether or not it's clean and shiny or dirty and ragged. Unlike the real world, the social, political, and economic context is rarely reflected in the imagined technology.

---

[1] http://thearchdruidreport.blogspot.com/2014/02/fascism-and-future-part-three-weimar.html

All of this, at the end of the day, makes for a very rote and dull genre unless your eyes endlessly light up at any sign of space travel. Not that I don't enjoy myself some science fiction. The latest *Star Wars* was pleasantly diverting, I'm a big fan of *Firefly*—which at least adds some depth and complexity to its characters and cultural context while also showing plenty of worlds not dominated by mega cities—and, well . . . I find the imagined travels throughout space somewhat fun! Yet there are only so many times you can rehash the same endless vision of the future before it becomes dull and lifeless—unless, of course, it feeds directly into an emotional need to believe in that exact sort of future.

I can't make claim to that need. Whenever I read some article waxing on about going to Mars, spouting the latest bit of tripe about NASA's supposed impending manned mission there or the Mars One lunacy, I can't help but wonder why the hell anyone would want to go. Judging by the pictures, it's beautiful in and of itself as a planet. I would hardly deny that description to any product of our universe, which by all accounts is mighty impressive both as creation and creator. But I will take an oak tree, a murmuring creek, a chicken poking through the grass, a goat dining on blackberry leaves, a cool rain, a flowering brassica, flitting birds, a good book, leaning against a loved one, a damn fine cup of coffee, the singing of frogs, or any of a thousand other experiences and sensations found only here at home (i.e. Earth) over the dry, dusty, lifeless and inhospitable red planet. *Humans don't belong there.* And that isn't an admission of defeat, it's a statement of a simple and relieving fact. It would take untold billions of dollars, god only knows how many man hours, and an essentially immoral amount of energy to get humans to the planet, if it's even possible, at which point they would almost certainly die in due time. And I doubt much time would be due. Why is this a goal?

I do not understand a desire to leave this planet. It's far too nice here and I am far too much a product of millions of years of an evolutionary dance with all the creatures and forces and life of *this planet* to want to go to another one—particularly one in which that co-evolutionary dance has likely not even begun. I do not take comfort or any particular joy in lifeless landscapes, no matter how stark and impressive they may be. I like mine filled with life, and there are so many here on this planet that I could never explore them all before I died.

There is the rub, the important and too-often-unspoken truth: circling around the endless rehashes of space travel and alien lifeforms, mega cities and computerized everything, is an endless number of likely and fascinating future scenarios right here on Earth that have gone unexplored. I can walk out my door into an array of compelling experiences and sensations, of life's ongoing stories in so many forms, and all I have to do is look. All I have to do is watch my chickens or talk to my neighbors, bend down and part the grass, take a short walk over to those flowering brassicas and discover the hundreds of pollinators—not just or even primarily the familiar honey bee, but a multitude of native insects I sadly don't even recognize or have names for—or even just look out upon the forested hillside (which will always be a better view than anything on Mars) and a thousand stories await me. They are everywhere, and these are the same kinds of stories that litter our coming future. They are ones rooted in our planet, in our soil, flowering out from the ecosystems that sustain us and the ones we're busy altering and degrading at every turn. All those actions of ours, all those choices that you and I make every day, are busy sculpting our future, and it isn't spaceships or holodecks or transporters that it's sculpting from the raw material of our ecological transgressions. It's climate change and resource depletion and industrial decline and—most of all—it's a wide variety of adaptive lifestyles lived right here, not out somewhere else in the universe. It's all the vagaries of human existence, good and bad, in an era of decline and collapse and, most critically, consequence.

I've said it time and again and will until I die: I expect the future to be harsh. But I also expect it to be fascinating and joyous and beautiful and worth it, no matter what, even if and when it feels like an unending string of cruelties. This is due to one simple expectation: that at the end of the day, whatever the future brings, I will live it right here on this planet I call home, within the ecosystems that have forged and created me and all the life around me, and open to the experience and sensations that come every day with the privilege of being alive on Earth. There is no better place to be. And a future *right here* is one worth imagining, even if it's littered with the consequences of our collective terrible decisions. Not only is it worth imagining, but it's necessary, because we cannot deal well with a future that we don't expect and can't imagine. We need the sort of stories found here in these pages, both to prepare us for the harsh future that we have so far largely failed to imagine, but also to remind us of the beauty of our home and the debt we owe it. Let us expect a life lived here and embrace it with all the excitement and anticipation we have granted imagined lives lived elsewhere. By placing ourselves and our futures firmly on the earth, we recognize its central importance and, gods willing, move one step closer to living right upon it and sensing the futures, in all their grace and cruelty and beauty, that now are forming around us.

- Nehalem, Oregon
April 22, 2016
Earth Day

Into the Ruins is published quarterly by Figuration Press. We publish speculative fiction that explores a future defined by natural limits, energy and resource depletion, industrial decline, climate change, and other consequences stemming from the reckless and shortsighted exploitation of our planet, as well as the ways that humans will adapt, survive, live, die, and thrive within this future.

One year, four issue subscriptions to *Into the Ruins* are $39. You can subscribe by visiting www.intotheruins.com or by mailing a check made out to Figuration Press to:

Joel Caris / 40100 Highway 53 / Nehalem, OR 97131

To submit your work for publication, please visit intotheruins.com/submissions or email submissions@intotheruins.com.

All issues of *Into the Ruins* are printed on paper. Electronic versions will be made available as time permits. In other words, it's not our top priority. But we do recognize it as particularly helpful for our international readers. The opinions expressed by the authors do not necessarily reflect the opinions of Figuration Press or *Into the Ruins*. Except those expressed by Joel Caris, since this is a sole proprietorship. That said, all opinions are subject to (and commonly do) change. This is due usually to the imperfect nature and fallibility of human beings—but also sometimes to wisdom.

EDITOR-IN-CHIEF
JOEL CARIS

ASSOCIATE EDITOR
SHANE WILSON

DESIGNER
JOEL CARIS

WITH THANKS TO
SHANE WILSON
JOHN MICHAEL GREER
OUR SUBSCRIBERS

SPECIAL THANKS TO
KATE O'NEILL

CONTRIBUTORS

JOEL CARIS is a gardener and homesteader, occasional farmer, passionate advocate for local and community food systems, sporadic writer, voracious reader, sometimes prone to distraction and too attendant to detail, a little bit crazy, a cynical optimist, and both deeply empathetic toward and frustrated with humanity. He is your friendly local editor and publisher. As a reader of this and hopefully future editions of *Into the Ruins*, he hopes you don't too easily tire of his voice and perspective. He lives in Oregon with an amazing, endlessly patient woman who likely is better than he deserves.

N.N. SCOTT spent his early years in Texas, where he engaged in (what the minister in *The Big Chill* eloquently called) "a seemingly random series of occupations." He spent most of the last decade serving overseas but hopes, if all goes well, to return to his beloved homeland before long. He has had scholarly work published in the *Southwestern Historical Quarterly*, fiction in one of the *Writers of the Future* volumes, and is, alas, working on a novel.

J. SHAMBURGER is a member of the International Society of Oilfield Trash, grandfather, sustainable farmer and CollapseNik, currently surviving in suburbia while retreating with extreme prejudice to the farm. His hobbies include extreme wood turning, wine making, mentoring and the divine southern pursuits of fishing and hunting. His work in oil and gas drilling has taken him throughout the world. One son is a lawyer and another his farming partner. One daughter a sommelier and another a weaver. His patient spouse coaches for USA Swimming. His recent hip replacement will, with luck, put him back in the tractor seat soon.

CATHERINE MCGUIRE is a writer/artist with a deep interest in Nature, both human and otherwise. Recent short stories have appeared in three volumes of *After Oil* (Founders House Publishing). Her poetry chapbook, *Palimpsests*, was published by Uttered Chaos in 2011 and her first full-length book of poetry, *Elegy for the 21st Century*, will be published by Future-Cycle Press in 2016. She has three self-published chapbooks.

G. KAY BISHOP is the author of the Gladdis of Rowanswood series[1] and creator of many fictional worlds. Works in process include the celebrated intuitive detective Shirleik Hollmer (with her roommates Dr. Wattsdotter and the glum inventor Meckinberg), the Many Nations post-industrial age story series, and a contemporary pastiche of Jane Austen wherein the women are rich and the men are not[2]. A community-supported artist, Bishop hopes *Into the Ruins* revitalizes the tradition of serial magazine print format for conserving low-tech and small-ag nonfiction as well as good storytelling.

W. JACK SAVAGE is a retired broadcaster and educator. He is the author of seven books, including *Imagination: The Art of W. Jack Savage* (wjacksavage.com). To date, more than fifty of Jack's short stories and over seven hundred of his paintings and drawings have been published worldwide. Jack and his wife Kathy live in Monrovia, California. Jack is responsible for this issue's cover art.

TONY F. WHELKS is the fiction-only pen name of a fifty-something writer living in the rural East Midlands of England. Initially trained as a pharmacist, he has worked in electronics, communications and renewable energy, then spent some years as an activist with a variety of environmental NGOs. He is also an amateur radio operator and permaculture gardener. His fiction was first published in the satirical periodical "Guernsey Attic Press" in the 1990s, but writes nonfiction newspaper and magazine articles under his real name.

JUSTIN PATRICK MOORE, KE8COY, is a writer, radio hobbyist and student of the Mysteries. His work has been published in *Flurb*, *Witches and Pagans*, and *Abraxas: International Journal of Esoteric Studies*. His post-collapse novelette *Water In the Dry Land* is available free on his website sothismedias.com where he blogs about dreams, magic, art and culture in the age of industrial decline. Justin and his wife make their home in Cincinnati, the Queen of the West.

---

[1] http://gkaybishop.weebly.com/chapter-files.html
[2] http://gkaybishop.weebly.com/checks-and-balances.html

LETTERS TO THE EDITOR

Dear Editor,

Writing about the future . . .

The future is the target of the arrows of the present. They don't always fly where we aim them, sometimes a bulls eye, sometimes an outer ring, sometimes missing the target altogether, sometimes looping around against all expectations and striking us in the butt.

The future rarely turns out as we expect it to be. It's like looking through a window of wavy glass; it moves and shifts as we change our perspective. "If present trends continue . . ." is a pleasant exercise, but they rarely do. There's often something that mucks up the works, throws the wheels off the track, drops a monkey wrench into the works. "No one expects the Spanish Inquisition."

There are commonalities in human societies, human characteristics that we have struggled with as long as we have been human: the needs of the group versus the desires of the individual, incest, resource distribution, population control, support for the nonproductive (elderly and infants), access to sex, power and control. These will always be a part of future human societies as long as there are enough humans left to gather together in groups.

What would a future human story tell us about balancing these very real human attributes in a world of declining resource availability, drug resistant bacteria, reduced energy, increased social tensions, increased wealth and power disparity, decline of national governments, and corporate and military domination struggling to control the remaining energy resources?

Two worlds, with humans pulled between the remainder of the human built world of power and control, and the diminishing natural world of cooperation, natural limits and cycles.

Could there be a balance, a dynamic equilibrium in a natural human world with struggling enclaves of technocracy, or are they forever hopelessly at odds with each other, incompatible, oil and water that can never mix?

Michael A. Lewis
Santa Cruz, California

Dear Editor,

I'm excited about the prospects of digging *Into the Ruins*. I have a feeling the vein of ideas tapped into by the stories you'll be publishing will become a treasured resource for those of us who are seeking to weave new narratives into the braid of history. Readers and writers have grown weary of the tired tropes that continue to duel for dominance in tales about the future. The post-human techno-dreams and post-apocalyptic wastelands of mass market publishing have become barren fields; just adding chemical fertilizer to them does not produce a better crop of stories. Trying to draw sustenance out of soil that has been stripped of vital nutrients has many downsides, possible starvation included. As Barry Lopez pointed out in his book *Crow and Weasel,* "sometimes a person needs a story more than food to stay alive. That is why we put these stories in each other's memories. This is how people care for themselves." The futures the writers chronicle in the pages of this quarterly have an opportunity to nourish a perspective of cultural experimentation and bricolage missing from the commonplace records now available off the shelf. In a world made by hand, off the shelf answers to the predicaments of the age won't be forthcoming. As industrial civilization unravels, the collective yarns society has been spinning about itself will have to be untangled and looked at with fresh eyes. I look forward to receiving the scoop from those visionaries brave enough to field reports from an epoch as yet uncharted. With grace and courage I also hope to contribute stories of my own.

Justin Patrick Moore
Cincinnati, Ohio

Dear Editor,

As the child of a mother who constantly took her two young boys to the public library and who would buy them pretty much anything they wanted from those grade school Scholastic book orders, I grew up as a heavy reader. Not only that, but 99% of what I read was fiction.

As I reached my early teen years not only did I start religiously watching *Star Trek: The Next Generation* on TV, but through a friend ended up getting hooked on *Star Trek: TNG* novels (which ended up superseding pretty much all of my other reading). And not only did I own several dozen of those novels, but I also noticed the uncomfortable reality that the anticipation of *buying* the next book actually gave me more pleasure than actually *reading* it. Reading for me had become little more than part of a materialist, consumerist trap.

As I got into my late teens I largely did away with reading books for watching films, partly because I was starting my post-secondary education and presumed career as a filmmaker. I fortunately ditched that after ten years, and upon deciding to no longer make the stuff I also decided I wasn't going to watch it either, and so haven't watched any film, television, or online video since 2006. And what has replaced that hole? Nothing but what I was doing all those years ago: reading books.

Fortunately, nothing of what I read nowadays involves transporters or food replicators. On top of that, things have swung in the opposite direction, and 99% of what I now read is nonfiction (the rare exception being Wendell Berry and Thomas Hardy novels).

I don't have much time or interest in reading fiction nowadays, and in particular have been averse to science fiction due to my false impression that it's all about warp drives and holodecks. But having read all of John Michael Greer's non-fiction peak oil books I decided to give his novels a chance last year and am glad to have discovered that not only is science fiction not just about spandex-clad, space-trotting colonialists, but that the perspectives and ideas offered in them can be quite rewarding and illuminating as well, particularly for this post-industrial / collapse era of ours. On top of that, not only can (science) fiction be a welcome relaxation from reading mounds of nonfiction, but, and I say this as someone who doesn't attend shows or watch any film or television, it can be seriously entertaining! (Perhaps I could now call post-industrial / collapse fiction my guilty pleasure.)

Along with reading two of John Michael Greer's novels and the first *After Oil* collection last year, I've recently started reading the weekly installments to Jason Heppenstall's online novel *Seat of Mars*, all of which I've thoroughly enjoyed. I don't need to tell you however that there is a serious dearth of post-industrial / collapse fiction out there, and so it's with much excitement—although not of the consumerist-trap *Star Trek: TNG* sort—that I look forward to reading *Into the Ruins* over the coming years, and which I preemptively thank you for your efforts.

Allan Stromfeldt Christensen
fromfilmerstofarmers.com
New Zealand

Dear Editor,

I'm not much of a country music fan, however I always enjoyed Kenny Rogers' song "The Gambler." The song tells a dark tale of a chance encounter between two guys on a train heading to nowhere. One of those two guys is The Gambler and he offers his companion, who is a bit down on his luck, a bit of friendly advice in return for a shot of whiskey. The Gambler then provides his hard won wisdom in the form of the classic lines from the song:

If you're gonna play the game, boy
You gotta learn to play it right

I'm no expert when it comes to complex topics such as peak oil, peak resources or even pollution. But I do know something about solar photovoltaic (PV) energy. What worries me is that nowadays a lot of people act like gamblers because they pretend to know a lot about solar PV energy, when they don't really know that much at all and haven't learned to play it right.

I built my own house here in this remote South Eastern corner of Australia and when it came time to think about connecting up the new house to the mains electricity grid, the cost was so crazy expensive that I thought to myself: *I'm not going to do that.* I had been using small scale solar PV and battery systems on a shed for a few years so instead of connecting the house up to the mains electricity grid, I just wired up a much larger version of the earlier system that I thought I knew so well.

Australia is a sunny place, no doubts about that. We've got a lot of sun. In fact we've got so much sun, that we've got the problem of too much sun. Really, there is a lot of sun down here.

What completely took me by surprise in the first year of living with an off grid solar PV system, was that for 3 weeks either side of the winter solstice (6 weeks in total), the sun was so low in the sky that I was lucky to generate more than one hour of charge on average from the solar PV panels in an entire day. It barely snows here, the winters are not particularly gloomy or cloudy either and to be honest, they're reasonably mild. I use very little energy most days anyway and have done so for a very long time (generally under 3.5kWh for the day) but in that first year I actually ran out of power. It was a bit of a shock (maybe pun intended).

Yet I constantly hear gamblers making crazy proclamations such as: We can power the current industrial civilisation purely on solar PV! From my perspective, that is pure crazy talk because based on my experience, it is simply not possible. I had to keep adding additional solar PV panels from the original 8 to the current 23 to my system until it generated more energy on average during that winter period than I was using. That eventually worked out to be 4.2kW of solar PV panels.

Thoughts of trying to charge an electric vehicle from an off grid solar PV system are completely ludicrous. Anyone that tries it will find that they are unable to. I'm only aware of one person on this entire continent who has actually tested that proposition and the guy has a huge off grid solar PV system, but is also able to draw additional energy from the mains grid! Electric vehicles nowadays consume between 0.17kWh and 0.25kWh per kilometre (0.27kWh and 0.4kWh per mile). Therefore my 4.2kW of solar panels would generate enough energy over winter to travel 17.5km (10.8 miles) and there would be no power left over for anything else. I'd also be worried if I had to drive up a hill or run the car heater or air-conditioner as that would further reduce the amount of distance that could be travelled. And gamblers say that solar powered electric vehicles are the way of the future, but I reckon they're smoking hopium (or their shorts)!

This solar PV system stuff isn't cheap either. Gamblers always say to me: "You're so lucky because you don't get an electricity bill and they're so expensive nowadays." Well, the panels themselves have actually come down in price over the past decade, but nothing else has and I doubt that it will. The solar PV system includes hundreds of metres (feet) of cables, multiple battery charge controllers, fuses, and a very complex inverter (far more expensive than the dumb sort of inverters seen in grid tied solar PV systems). Not to mention the batteries themselves. None of that stuff is getting cheaper and setting up a small off grid solar PV system is like paying for 50 years of electricity bills up front, but gamblers generally forget that bit as they only ever see the wins and ignore the losses.

People always love to show me their smart phones and say how small they are. I don't have one of those smart phones, but I can agree with people that they are small and seem to be getting smaller. Gamblers build on that story and then proceed to tell me how advanced the battery technology is and how they are getting cheaper, as well as smaller, every year. Yet from what I see, those same batteries barely power that smart phone device for longer than a day. And you'd be lucky to get two years lifespan out of the batteries before they are unable to hold a charge. The batteries here have a lifespan of somewhere between 15 and 25 years and despite what you've heard, batteries are a very old and very mature technology. Great advances in battery technology may be possible, but I wouldn't be gambling my savings on those advances happening any time soon.

I want to end this letter to the editor by discussing limits. We live in a society where it is almost heretical to suggest that limits exist. Certainly gamblers would never discuss limits. It is worthwhile noting that an off grid solar PV system imposes strict limits on a household including:

- There are only so many appliances that can be turned on at once;
- There is only so much stored energy in the batteries;
- The batteries have an upper limit as to the amount of energy they can supply regardless of how much total energy is stored;
- If the air temperature exceeds about 25'C (77'F) the solar panels produce less and less energy as they get ever hotter;
- If the sun isn't shining strongly and high in the sky, then your system is not generating much energy at all;
- The more stress you put your solar PV system under, the shorter its lifespan will be; and
- It can be difficult running garden lights during long winter evenings.

Chris McLeod
Victoria, Australia

Dear Editor,

I recently had to replace the pull cord on a Briggs/Stratton generator. Sounds simple, right?

Pulling the air cleaner off the carb, I was faced with two Torx-like screw heads. I say "Torx-like," as they resembled Torx, but were asymmetrical. I used vise-grips, ruined the screws and replaced with Phillips head screws.

The cowling had both ANSI and metric bolts retaining it, of three different sizes. I replaced those with all ANSI of the same size.

The pull cord cover was riveted into the cowling, requiring replacement of the entire cowling when the pull cord broke, for a mere $125 plus shipping plus waiting a week. I drilled out the rivets and replaced with screws, after winding the new cord in.

There were two bolts securing nothing on the cowling—I have no idea why. There was a switch without connection to anything except a ground point. I have no idea why that switch existed. There were plastic bolts retaining the air cleaner—which disintegrated when I tried to reassemble the airbox after the repair—I replaced with steel Phillips screws.

While the generator was there, I decided to change the oil—and discovered the oil drain plug was made of some cheap pot metal—and the plug stripped when using a wrench, stripped more when vise-grips were applied, and finally had me drilling a hole and using an EZ-Out to remove the plug remnants without damaging threads.

Replaced that with an ANSI bolt as well.

Now, I am NOT average. I can fix almost anything, from a handloom to rebuilding a truck motor, and certainly a broken pull cord. But I can tell you that if ever I met the group of idiots that designed this generator, I would most certainly pull my can of Whup-Ass out and use it quite liberally.

J. Shamburger
Deep Woods of East Texas

Into the Ruins *welcomes letters to the editor from our readers. We encourage thoughtful commentary on the contents of this issue, the themes of* Into the Ruins, *and humanity's collective future. Insightful, concise, entertaining, unique, and unexpected letters of preferably 500 words or less (though, as one can see, this is not a hard limit) are appreciated. Readers may email their letters to editor@intotheruins.com, or send by mail to:*

Into the Ruins
c/o Joel Caris
40100 Highway 53
Nehalem, OR 97131

Please include your full name, city and state, and an email and phone number. Published letters will include your full name and location but your other contact information will be kept strictly confidential.

STORIES

THE SPECIALIST
BY J. SHAMBURGER

"Da, is it true that when you were a kid lectricity was all over?" Janet's lithe fingers flicked the defunct light switch rhythmically. At fourteen, she was gawky, clumsy, and a complex buzzsaw of energy searching for an outlet. Her eyes flitted about the tiny room I called an office.

"Yes it was," I replied, "even down to the river there was lectricity. It ran all down wires hung between the road poles, and all you had to do was connect the wires to your house. And pay for it, of course."

"And there was TeeVees that made movies in every house? What's a movie really, Da? I bet it's like a giant TeeVee, huh? Just takes lotsa lectricity and that's why we only can go to the one in town." She honestly never stopped, and yet her sister was equally as hard to start. Both of them finished well, though, no matter the activity, and that was important.

"Hunny, there was so much lectricity that lotsa folks had a TeeVee in every room, each one showing a different movie. Leastways, that's what Grandad said."

"That's sooo hunky Da! Was it lotsa coppers for the lectricity?"

"Janet! Your turn to wash the dishes—get your butt in here!" My daughter Summer, sweet as she was, had the vocal chords of a ships' first mate. My granddaughter cringed, and swiveling her neck around, grinned at me while her eyes rolled back.

"Gotta go, Da!" rushed out of her, as her feet thumped the floor my father and I had made so many years ago.

I could hear the rustle-rustle-clack-clack of her twin, June, working the big loom upstairs. I still wasn't sure if the loom in the house was a good idea, but it beat building a new shed just for the weaving. My hands were cramped from writing, and I suddenly wished we had the money for a typewriter and ink ribbon. Now that was tek that made sense, not the crazy steam generator they were working on at the school. Why did they think that it was necessary for a barn size machine just to run old tek that broke after a few months? Even lectric lantern bulbs were nigh on impossible to buy these days, and most homesteads had sold their copper years ago.

I gathered up the drawings Summer had made over this last year. She was a talented artist and very detailed. I was amazed at her ability to copy the crumbling drawings in Gray's Anatomy, interpreting even the tiny textures of the faded printing into shades and colors that seemed alive again. Until she volunteered, I had no idea that she was capable of this, and I treasured each panel she completed.

I placed the papers in a cloth pouch and slipped them into the desk, looking for my key to the work drawer. It was the only way to be sure none of the kids or assorted friends would put grimy paws on those expensive sheets, much as I hated to lock anything away. I was truly thankful that we had paper once again, but longed for the school to get the printing press running. I put the colored illustrating pencils in the drawer as well, knowing they were just too tempting for little hands and minds.

I dimmed the lamp, as I intended coming back into work shortly. Gingerly, I eased out the back door, pulling up on the handle so the hinges didn't squawk. I could hear the girls in the kitchen arguing over who was going to fetch eggs and who was going to feed pigs and horses.

The stars were out in full force, the Milky Way pushing the deep darkness back into the undergrowth. In a few seconds my eyes were right and I walked down toward the road. Our lone remaining telephone pole stood erect like a rooster tail, the Maker banner waving lazily in sometimes wind. The Weaver and Hosteler banners were barely moving, as if unsure of the wind. *Wind must be higher up tonight*, I thought. The lowest banner remained unmoved, the red of it now black in the starlight.

Walking by the blueberry trees hemming the base, I wondered when that last telephone pole would finally rot. Then we would need to do like everyone else, and put our banners on the fence or gate. But for now, I was glad the old pole was still there, like me—too stubborn to roll over and give up.

I didn't miss the lectricity as much as I thought I would. It was a lot of work just trying to make enough to pay for it, and then you couldn't afford to buy much that was lectric anyway. The biggest pain was still washing clothes, but the crank washer didn't take long and the newer model with the pull-down lever action was so much easier to pump. It just made more sense to let the lectricity go, because we gained much more time not trying to pay the lectric bill, and it really cost a lot to keep the old tek working.

That new crank mechanism made my father rush into my mind, replete with creaky nasal voice and bad hip, making him list when he walked. He would so be bitching about no refrigeration and the dearth, and finally death, of instant ice.

Had to have that ice for his bourbon, as harsh as it was coming out of his old still. I remembered the gray-shot beard and the scars, so very many scars all over him, each one an adventure in itself.

"Gravity is a bitch son. Whenever you design something, make sure the Gravity Bitch is on your side!" I smiled, missing him and his unbelievable ability to make something from nothing, to reduce complex problems to basic things anyone could understand. "There is only one way a man can eat a monster, son . . ." and he would look at me as I finished it, chiming in just right so our voices merged: "one bite at a time!" And then there was the laughter and the feeling of him, and I missed both in an achy way inside.

I turned into the road, remembering how not many years ago this would have been crazy, me walking alone down this lumpy asphalt, without a gun and several people to watch front and rear. I remembered cars and trucks of my early youth, and the amazing tek of the Online, lectricity everywhere just by flipping a switch. And looking up, I recalled rarely seeing stars and not even knowing where the Bear or the Archer was in the night sky. I missed it some, the lectricity, but not enough. The Harrisons' lights were on far down the road and high atop the tallest hill in the county. Their generator, older than I am, ran on most anything liquid, even if it did smoke a lot. That bright lectric light just looked unnatural to me after these last few years—it now looked cold and wasteful, and to me it was both.

I turned about, intent on going away from that cold light, and headed east towards the Ramos house. I could just see the lamp glow through their front window. Ellie and Rosa would be doing dishes, same as in my house. I could hear horses thumping off in the pasture, likely running under the starlight.

"Da!" I jumped at my older sons voice, having been lost in my thoughts a little too much. "Old man, you trying to stir up trouble? The wife sent me to find you."

"I'm old son, not feeble minded. But I do admit to a certain frailty in the hip."

"Yea—you walk like Grandad now, you know? It's almost like seeing him when I walk up on you, only your limp is on the left and not the right." I could see teeth behind his smile, bright beneath starlight.

"You want me to walk with you some?" I could smell grease and iron tang on him from the workshop, and there was wine on his breath.

"Sure son. You get into that fig wine or is that the blackberry?"

"Oh no—I'm not touching that fig. It's worth too much at market nowadays. Blackberry for me."

I chuckled, remembering us opening the first bottle of fig wine years back, and drinking it. We had looked at each other as we spat it out, him not wanting to tell me it tasted like ass and me not wanting to admit the same. We didn't say anything, just laughed together as I poured the bottle out. But I hadn't been able to throw out six cases of hard work, so I put the batch back into the root cellar and left it.

Spring cleaning two years later, his wife had found it. We opened a bottle, and the smell was amazing. We each took a nip from the bottle. The both of them had looked at me, and my daughter-in-law said, "Please tell me you kept the recipe for this?"

"Yep," was my glib and happy reply.

"Oh yeah!! Where is the rest of this stuff, Da?" my son asked.

I pointed to the back of the cellar and couldn't stop the grin creasing my face. I reached out and took the open bottle, spinning it in my hand to look at the cloth label. It had seemed a waste to make those labels back then, yet now they were prized within the county and even further afield from our farm. "Figaros Blessing" wine went for two silvers a bottle now, and as we had the only fig trees in the area, it had become a "thing" for the local fair and a guaranteed copper stream, as long as we kept the recipe in the family and didn't sell the fig saplings.

We had walked just a little ways towards the warmer light, when my son reached out and grasped me by the elbow. "You hear that Da?"

I listened, but my old ears were not his. "Nope. What is it?"

"Horses, Da. Two or three, maybe four." Without any urging, I eased down into the ditch along the road, pulling him into deeper darkness between burgeoning branches of scrub. We waited silently and unmoving.

A luminescence appeared at the rise in the road, and then a light. The horse hooves did not waiver in their rhythm, determined but not crazed. My son was peering intently at the group. I did not even try, knowing full well that my eyesight wasn't up to that task.

"It looks like the Warden. It's a palomino, and he has one of 'em." A few more seconds, and then he moved out of the darkness. "Yea Da, it's the Warden and two more."

I followed him to the road, and he strode into the middle of it. As the light and men approached, they reined in, horses blowing, their shivering withers slinging sweat.

"Evening folks," he said. His eyes glanced across my son as he touched his hand to the brim of his hat. Then they landed on me.

"Old Da, we have need of you. Had an accident over at the school with the steam boiler. There are kids hurt bad, and some others too."

The bottom fell out of my stomach. I did not want this, not tonight. But there it was, and I was the only one. "How many?" I asked.

"Two for certain need you, from what I can see. The others, well, its best you just come with us." I then noticed the fourth horse, a black, behind Bill Morning and his Big Red. Bill nudged the horse forward, and tossed me the reins.

"Please Da, boots up. We have the need and you are the only one," said Bill. His eyes were intent on me, his horse restless and fussing a little back and forth. Big Red was sensing the anxiety of each of them, evident in his many head bobs and prancing steps.

I grabbed the saddlehorn, and pulled, throwing my bad hip over the back of the black. "I'll need some things," I said. Tugging the reins, I headed the black towards our farm and the lone telephone pole.

As I pulled into the yard, I called out. "Summer! June!"

The screen door squeaked open, and June was there with a lamp. "You needed, Da?" was all she asked.

"Yep. Would you get my bag?"

She returned in a few seconds, and handed me the small, red leather satchel. I slung it over my shoulder. "Be back when I can. Love to you all." I eased back on one rein, then clucked and nudged the black in the flanks. He wheeled in a tight turn and the two of us merged into the darker starlit night, the others in my wake. We passed my son, who stood at road's edge, watching.

We rode for the half hour or so it took to get to the school. There wasn't any fire, but there were very many lamps, hung from hooks near doorways or simply set on the ground or on top of crates along the side of the building. Wood scraps and pieces of timber and splinters were everywhere. There was a lot of water puddling and gathering into pools, and my black splashed it over a few people as I reined him in.

A hand reached up and grasped the rein on one side of my black. I looked down into the face of a girl, no more than eighteen or twenty. "You're needed in this building Da. Needed bad, too," she said. She had very obviously been crying, and seeing me brought more tears to her young cheeks.

The old adage "up with the good, down with the bad" ran through my head as it did every time I left level ground these days. I eased my bad leg down gingerly, holding the saddlehorn like a drowning man. I felt my foot touch the solid earth below, and then let the reins fall into the young girl's hands.

She looped them around the stakes on a nearby wagon. "Hurry Da! Please!"

I went into the building, and saw a young man stretched out on a table, unmoving. Two other young men stood close to him.

I strode over, my heart thudding in my chest. His lower jaw was missing, shreds of meat and connective tissue dangling over the gaping maw where his smile had once been. Blood oozed from the ragged torn flesh, slowly forming tiny pools on the table below the boy's shoulders. We had been long enough on the road that clotting was well along.

I could look right into his throat beneath the upper teeth and his palate. The glaring white rings of his trachea made my stomach churn. I felt sick rising in me, knowing the pain and fear this young boy would be in should he awaken. He breathed wetly through the end of the exposed trachea, but thankfully unconscious.

"His folks or family here?" I asked those next to me.

"He's my brother, Da," said one of the boys. "He's a goner, ain't he?" The boy had red-rimmed eyes and tear streaks tracked down his cheeks between the grime.

"Yes. You're right about that. Did you say any goodbyes?"

"No, Da. No time. He's been out since the explosion," came the whispery reply.

"We aren't waiting for your folks, son. I don't want him waking up and knowing this ugliness. Take your brother's hand, and be with him now in his need."

The boy took a step, then grasped his brother's hand. I cradled the injured head in my arm, and took the long-corded knife from beneath my shirt. Right at the juncture of his collarbone, I slid it home and made a wiggle or two or three beneath the pallid young man's skin. I felt the wash of his blood spill over my hand, and laid his head gently back on the table. I held the dying boy's free hand, the brother and I letting his spirit slip away peacefully.

As the blood slowed to a trickle, I heard the breath slowing. Thankfully there was no gurgling or spasms. He just left quickly into the starlit night.

"Say what words you will, son. He has one foot on another path right now, and soon he will leave us forever."

Others gathered close now, and one voice started as others joined it in a soft, rhythmic wave.

"Mercy for you, brother. Mercy for your family. Mercy for us all," rolled out softly from the growing group.

"Mercy for you, brother. Mercy for your family. Mercy for us all."

I turned my back on his pain, on their grief, my own hard enough to bear. I hoped the young man hadn't been conscious of his injury. It was traumatic and crippling, and he would have felt every bit of that injury down to his soul.

I forced my own feelings aside, and began looking about for others. There was another knot of people, obviously struggling to hold someone down. I quickly strode to that table, and the people parted to let me close.

A woman was there; her now-partial face and most of her upper body had sagging, bright red flesh, some pieces grayish white. Her arms were gray below the elbows, and I noted muscle movements only in her upper arms. Her struggles were feeble, and she knew she was a goner as well. It was evident in her eyes.

"I'm here, sister. I'm here," I said. She ceased struggling somewhat, but it was obvious there was no surcease to be obtained, no matter how she contorted herself.

"Oh please Da! Pleeze let me go!" She thrashed violently, her ragged cries echoing in the quiet of the room. She looked in my eyes, and I felt the person that was *her*, even if I did not know her close. A Da knows these looks, knows what they each mean and knows the weight of them. I heard the mercy chant sonorous behind me, and reached into my bag.

"Ooohhh pleeeze Da!! Pleeeze!" She was trying to cry but couldn't, not with the pain. One of her cries skirled up into a scream.

I held her head with one hand. "Grab her tight once more," I instructed the others. Their grips tightened, and I poured a full half-cup of poppy milk into her swollen mouth. She didn't look to be swallowing much, and I tried to massage her throat, but the tissue was too loose from the scalding and burns. I poured more, until she choked on it.

"Let her be for now," I said. "Is there any family?"

An older woman pushed to the fore. "She's mine, Da. My daughter-in-law."

"Where is her husband?" I asked, looking into her stoic face. She was one who held it all in for later, or maybe forever. I didn't know which. The cries had risen into wails behind me. I cringed at each one, trying not to physically flinch, to be strong for those with need.

"He's two days from here, working at the mill in Groveton. I'll stand with her Da, to be sure." She walked up and grasped her daughter-in-law's hand, but there was no response. The wails had stopped, and the injured woman was fading, her thrashing declining.

"Touch her shoulder Ma'am. I don't think she can feel your hand," I instructed her.

A faraway look began in her eyes. She calmed as she saw her relative and felt the touch on her shoulder.

"Stay with her and see her off. Make sure she knows you're here and let her see the love you have," I said. Everyone around the table nodded slowly, not quite in unison. I heard the final echoes of the mercy chant at the other table, and looked up. Those were now coming here as well. Soon the mercy chant would begin anew.

In full Da mode now, I walked onward, seeing obviously injured people surrounded by one or two others for support or care. I pushed what I had just done away, down deep, and summoned logic to the fore of my mind. Here was a simple burn, the blister already formed, covering the outside of a young girl's lower arm. I pricked it to let the fluid out, and applied an oily burn poultice from the First Aid kit, scattered across a table. I grabbed a large bottle marked "Sterile Saline" and another labeled "Alcohol" from the littered medical supplies.

A hirsute man had a deep vertical gash in his arm, just between bicep and tricep muscles. I could see arterial pulsing in the base of the wound. *Lucky man, this one*, I thought. I washed the assorted dirt and clots from the wound with sterile saline solution.

"This is going to hurt like hell," I warned him. "I need to make sure it's sterile before I close your wound." I looked around, the rhythmic chanting echoing in my head, filling my sensorium. I pushed it away and focused.

"You!" I pointed as I raised my voice. A young man in his late teens or thereabouts looked back at me. "Come over here." He walked over without reply, looking at my face. I wondered what he saw.

"Hold his shoulder with one hand and his wrist with the other," I instructed. He did, but had placed himself squarely in my way.

"Get behind him, and switch hands." He complied, and I looked into a pair of dark, nearly black eyes. "Hold that shoulder down, and his hand flat on the table." The young man braced both his arms, holding downward, firmly.

I looked at the bristly arm of the injured man, then into his pallid face. "Your singular job is not to move that arm." I placed a wad of cloth bandage in his mouth. "Bite this and try not to scream," I warned. Without any lapse, I poured alcohol into the gash.

He grunted, and the grunt turned into a deep moan as his eyes turned to the ceiling and his arm spasmed. The younger man continued to hold the wounded arm tightly at both wrist and shoulder. I mentally counted to five, then rinsed with the saline. I had no idea what had sliced the man, but with all the metal I had seen, tetanus was a distinct possibility. The hairy man relaxed a little, and I threaded my suturing needle with gut. Thirty-nine stitches later, I applied an orange peel poultice over the sutures.

I told the younger man to find some cloth and make a sling. As he departed in search of cloth, and I finished wrapping my work, the sonorous chanting crept back into my skull.

"Be sure and give that poultice two days, then wash the stitches with clean boiled water. Get it into sunlight and aired out after that. If it weeps, and it likely will, then keep it washed with sterile water. Get by my homestead in three days, no later."

Dully, he nodded his head. "Aye Da, I'll do all that."

I moved on to a woman seated in a chair, a flap of her scalp ripped free and hair matted in the wound. I started towards her, forcing my mind to clarity and the many tasks at hand.

One at a time, I treated them. Not always as I wanted, but always as best I could, with what I had.

It was a long night. Three were let go down the path and beyond. That was my job, to set them on the path and ease their letting go. For the rest, they will heal. Maybe not exactly as they once were, for scars are facts of healing and there is only so much a Da can do.

I am not a judge of people.
I am not a finder of faults.

I am not a giver of blessing.
I am not a doer of miracles.

As I climbed onto the black horse in the morning sun, my red leather bag hit my thigh. I looked down at it, the smallness of it. I remembered my youth in the bright shiny corridors of Memorial Hospital. Inside I railed at so many things, so very many things now lost to us.

There were things in every one of my diagnostic books that no longer existed, but which were considered daily items in a hospital or in a doctor's cupboard. Those things had already been lost when I apprenticed at Memorial, yet the books infuriatingly referred to them as if they grew on trees like pears.

Even sterility was assumed. Yet sterility was hard to come by, and took time that wasn't always available. So many I had let go just because my choice was to close the wound and hope, or let them bleed out and take their path. And yet the faded surgical books showed methods to transplant organs!

I wondered what the world had been like in my Grandad's time. When every broken body could be fixed and infection healed with a pill, did it make people act and think differently? Did they feel as invulnerable as they nearly were? But then again, that was the old days and this was my reality. Wishing for the past netted a man nothing. All I can do is try to better what we have, keep the things that matter straight and honest.

Solace for others is a part of my trade now.
I give what I can.
I do what I can.

Judge me as you will . . . judge me, but know that when you need it, mercy can be had.

I nudged the horse back towards my homestead and my writing.

AMERICAN SILVER
BY N.N. SCOTT

Samareh LaTrobe sat waiting with mud on her boots, in a tall chair of carved oak upholstered in faded red velvet, in a stone-walled chamber in the Government House of Manhattoes, the gloomy brownstone fortress that dominated the hilly northern edge of that island. At the far end of the room three high windows overlooked the Hudson, but the river was hidden in the late evening mists of October, and the dark glass reflected only slashes of yellow light from two small electroliers with dangling filament-wire bulbs that tried, and largely failed, to light the room. Government House was under the Admirate of Holy Commerce, and like all commercial spaces must be illuminated by electricity, but the rules didn't stipulate how well. Kerosene lamps were more common and would have done better, but none happened to be there. Samareh regarded the lights. The bulbs dazzled the eye so that the ceiling above them remained in shadow, a vague threatening space. Otherwise the room was furnished with a large ancient table of polished wood, other chairs like the one she occupied, and a couple of massive sideboards. There were no tapestries, and the rush matting on the floor had been worn to tatters. A typical waiting room; she had seen many. Samareh wore green canvas trousers with loaded side pockets, a forest green tunic with a dark red cloth belt and the insignia of her Detail pinned to the right sleeve, and a peaked cap with a red tassel. She took a long breath and let it out. Her back ached and her feet hurt, but work had to be done, in weariness or health.

A wooden door slid open and Jamsheed Morion entered, wearing the trim dark well-made suit of a Broker rumpled by a day's work. He carried a leather folder thick with papers and looked much as she remembered him from her student days, though older and more angular, the brown waxy skin of his face suffused by a net of fine wrinkles that converged around the eyes. After the typical formal greeting between a Broker and a Detail Officer he took a nearby seat, set his folder on the table and smiled. "I asked the Enforcement Detail to send someone who would be good in a pinch. I hardly expected to see my most promising student from back in Albany. You'll forgive an old man's awkward reminiscences."

Samareh smiled also. "There's nothing to forgive. I only hope that girl has managed to live up to some of her promise."

"No doubt of that." He scanned her insignia. "So you've found your way into Auditing and Reclamation."

She laughed a little. "Found my way. Something like that. In reality it's more like 'other duties as assigned.'"

"The better grade of people always end up doing that, and bless them for it. Well, to business." He opened the folder. "You will have time to review this on the way, so I'll make it short. I regret that we must meet under these circumstances, but there is a situation that requires both discretion and prompt action. A shipment containing seventeen hundred pounds of Jamaican coffee, a special variety much prized in certain quarters, has gone missing on its way to the consignment warehouse of Muckgrow and Nillie, in Pittsburgh. We need someone to locate it and get it to its destination, or to document the loss for an insurance claim."

"A significant problem," said Samareh, "but not one that would require involvement by an auditor. Something in your expression makes me think there's more to this."

"Of course. At the time of its disappearance the shipment was in care of two operatives, both young men on their first long-distance assignment, who have also vanished. One of them was Yasion Flowell."

Samareh, who had leaned over to scan the papers while he spoke, said, "The nephew of Master Lobard Gullen-Barange."

"Yes, on the Executive Board of Holy Commerce."

Samareh pondered his weary eyes, wondering whether her own looked any better. "And where did they go missing with this coffee?"

"We last heard from them in 'Arrisburg, preparing to trans-ship the bales onto the incline railroad that crosses the Blue Mountains. That was six weeks ago. Three weeks ago the Pittsburgh warehouse contacted us by short wave about the late delivery. As you can imagine, we have few trustworthy operatives in that region, but we reached an independent agent named Deering Culler, who made inquiries and learned nothing. It is as though they, and the coffee, vanished into air."

"'Arrisburg." Samareh frowned. "A large and wealthy town on the Suskehana River, but it's the seat of the Discordian religion. Holy Commerce has no official presence there. You suspect the Discordians?"

"Without evidence we can't suspect anyone, but some faction of Discordia may well be involved. Unfortunately there are five major sects, all differing from each other more than they do, in some ways, from other religions. Some are civilized pietists while others, according to rumor, are little more than crazed killers. It's not even clear whether 'religion' is the right term: their writings make little sense to outsiders." Jamsheed pushed the folder toward her. "You are requested to make your way to 'Arrisburg, investigate the matter and take whatever action seems appropriate."

Samareh nodded and picked up the file. "I'll get the next packet to Philadelphia and take the canal west from there. I can't help asking, why did those two operatives try to take this load by the southern route? They could have shipped it up the Hudson through Albany, then by the Great Canal to the lakes, and south to Pittsburgh by the western canals and the Ohio River."

Jamsheed crossed his hands before he spoke. "Yes, that would have been the normal route, until September. It's not public knowledge yet, but the Ohio Valley conflict has entered a new phase. The Conneaut and Shenango divisions of the western shipping canal have fallen into the hands of the Cleveland-Youngstown faction. As the steward of International Commerce, the Admirate remains neutral in such disputes."

"Of course," said Samareh.

"But despite our formal position of neutrality, it was thought best not to tempt fate by sending this shipment on the northern route. In my opinion coffee is nothing but black poison gruel, but it seems there is nothing so vile but someone will develop a taste for it. According to Muckgrow and Nillie, people out west trade furs of high quality in exchange for that stuff. It is the only thing that makes life bearable. Precious cargo attracts unwelcome attention."

"Then I'll be on my way." Samareh rose from her seat.

Jamsheed also stood. "Good luck to you, my friend, and may Saint Thatcher watch over your accounts."

In Philadelphia the weather was worse, with constant chilly rain and the streets swimming in mire, but she took time to visit the Franklin and Rose book hotel, an old and spacious building, every wall thick with bookshelves. The quiet, warm place smelled sweetly of old paper, old leather, lamp oil and wax. An elderly lady at the front desk introduced herself as Penny and after some polite chitchat about the rain, requested her membership card. Samareh handed over her Accounts & Reclamation ID, in its otterskin folder. "Ah, an A&R officer," said Penny with a prim smile as she passed the open card discreetly under a desktop magnifier to check the engraving. "We haven't had visitors from Commerce in a while. Do you need a study room for the night? Dinner's at seven bells."

"I'd love to stay, but I must read and go. I'm looking for information about the

Discordian Religion, as it's sometimes called."

"In that case let me show you to the catalog room, but I fear we might not have much in that line."

In the end, after thumbing through catalog cards and consulting several indexes chained to the desks, Samareh found a handwritten copy of the *Principia Discordia* bound in battered red leather, and a volume of Nedson's *Travels in Western Pennsylvania*, a standard work of the previous century. Penny brought them out from the back stacks and Samareh consulted them at a desk lit by the mingled light of the rainy afternoon through a four-paned window, and a kerosene desk lamp with a polished copper reservoir and green glass shade.

The *Principia* manuscript was unhelpful, apparently a student's transcript in difficult handwriting. What she could make of the text was whimsical and weird, littered with jargon and ribald passages that might have meant something to a reader of past centuries, but made little sense under the current circumstances. In one of its several so-called "introductions" she read:

> Organized religion preaches *Order* and *Love* but spawns *Chaos* and *Fury*. Why?
>
> Because the *whole Material Universe* is exclusive property of the Greco-Roman Goddess of *Chaos, Confusion, Strife, Helter-Skelter* and *Hodge-Podge*. No spiritual Power is even strong enough to dent Her Chariot Fenders. No material Force can resist the Temptation of Her Fifth Intergalactic Bank of the Acropolis Slush Fund for Graft and Corruption.
>
> All this was Revealed to me in an absolutely unforgettably miraculous event in 1958 or 1959, in a Bowling Alley in Friendly Hills or maybe Santa Fe Springs, California, witnessed by either Gregory Hill or Malaclypse the Younger or perhaps Mad Malik or Reverend Doctor Occupant or some Guy who must have vaguely resembled one or another of Them.

"Reverend Doctor Occupant?" she asked herself. "Fifth Intergalactic Bank? Malaclypse the Younger? And who is this goddess?" She returned to the catalog room, and in an encyclopedia found an entry on ancient Greek religion. Their goddess of chaos and strife was Eris, called Discordia by the Romans. The encyclopedia quoted Hesiod, an ancient author:

> This Eris, daughter of Night, stirs up even the shiftless to toil; for a man grows eager to work when he considers his neighbor's wealth, and neighbor vies with neighbor as he hurries after riches. This Strife is wholesome for men.

"Well, some things never change," she said. "Eris. 'Arrisburg. *Eris*-burg. Heh."
She took passage that night on a Union Canal barge heading west; it was slower

than a horse but for the first thirty miles the towpath was lighted and the barges moved at night, allowing her to sleep. The days passed. From Redding she took post horses, and from the small settlement at Hershey, nestled amid the melancholy ruins of its ancient splendor, she went by coach in the guise of a commercial traveler, in a plain wool suit, skirt and top coat. She arrived at the southern gate of 'Arrisburg on a chilly late October morning, under a sky the color of clay. The gate was surmounted by a Discordian symbol cast in old green bronze: the Five Fingered Hand of Eris, which somewhat resembled two arrowheads with curved flanges set against each other with their points touching, or more poetically, the crescent moon, horns pointed upward, rising over its reflected image with a horizon line between. Four guards stood by the archway wearing elaborate fancy dress uniforms of colored silk and silver braid, but they remained still as logs, blindfolded, with ropes tied around their hands and silken gags in their mouths. Two men came out of the gatehouse, both dressed as tatterdemalions in ragged clothes with their faces painted white and red. They carried automatic weapons of good quality. One of them leaned in the window and said:

> "She was not invited to the bash on Limbo Peak;
> So She threw the Golden Apple, 'stead of turn'd the other cheek!
> O it cracked the Holy Punchbowl and it made the nectar leak;
> Her Apple Corps is strong!"

Samareh looked back at him blankly, recognizing it as some kind of ceremonial greeting and wishing she'd had more time to consult *Travels in Western Pennsylvania*. Then the patent medicine drummer who shared the coach with her said, "Don't worry, I've done this before. It's part of the song of the Apple Corps. Just hold up your travel papers." To the guard he answered, in a singsong tone:

> "Rub-a-dub-dub-o!
> Hail Eris, Blessed Saint Hung Mung.
> Siya-Dastio!
> Hail Eris, Blessed Saint Mo-Jo."

The guard nodded, examined their papers, handed them back and said, "Welcome, guests, to the City of Luminations."

'Arrisburg stood within its walls, a wide semicircle along the eastern shore of the green Suskehana River, but the internal arrangements of the city were hard to comprehend. The sturdy many-roofed and many-gabled buildings were of gray local stone, their upper stories painted varying shades of ocher, dark blue, olive, burnt carmine and russet brown. The streets were narrow and except for a few ancient main roads they rambled in confusing ways. But five great paved courtyards opened, apparently at random, among the tangle. These—called Squares, though none were actually that shape—each surrounded or adjoined a large ceremonial building representing one of the five great Houses of Discordia. Their high domes and towers of patched and various design rose, pigeon-haunted, against the autumn sky, though the weathering of centuries had given them a solemn grandeur.

Samareh checked into an inn near the Square of the Apostles of Eris, and made efforts during that day to locate Deering Culler, the independent agent Jamsheed had mentioned. She had studied Culler's report before committing it to the fireplace of a Redding hotel, and in its vague yet erudite language she detected the intent of a deceiver. A personal interview might yield better information. The Discordians she met were affable, but inconveniently inclined to recite poetry, and she found their conversation hard to follow. After some delay she located Culler's boat, a thirty-foot, two-masted river freighter of squalid but serviceable appearance, at a small pier below Front Street. He stood on the landing, a stocky, energetic red-faced man with a tangle of damp white hair, directing his assistants who were unloading what looked like heaps of dirty broken pottery from the hold. Beyond them the river flowed, half a mile wide and studded with small tree-covered islands. To the north she could see the great highway bridge, built of timber on the stumps of its ancient pylons, and beyond that the dark slope of the Blue Mountains, more than a thousand feet high and thick with forest. Catching Culler's attention, she identified herself and began to explain her business, watching his face for signs of trouble. His eyes, as they roved up and down her figure while they spoke, suggested an unpleasant but ordinary kind of interest.

"Well now, it would be my pleasure to assist you," he said, smiling in a way that showed his front teeth, like a horse, "but I fear you've wasted your trouble." He repeated much of what she already knew from his report, adding that nothing more had been heard of the two commercial travelers. At his invitation she sat, somewhat uneasy, beside him on one of the large stones that lined the road, facing the boat so that Culler could oversee his workers, who were going about their task without enthusiasm. "Hop along there Mark!" he called in a louder voice. "Let's try to be done by nightfall, shall we?" Mark, a lanky figure in a checkered shirt, made a vague gesture in response. "You see what I have to deal with," Culler said.

"Are those two Discordians?"

Once again Culler made his little smirking smile. "You can't be serious, Samareh. I may call you Samareh, may I not? Yes. Well, Mark and Craine hail from much farther down the river, almost to New Baltimore. They're no Discordians, perish the thought."

"Do you think Discordians could be involved in this business of the missing men and their shipment?"

Culler's smirk was becoming annoying. "My dear, the Discordians could be involved in *anything*, and no one the wiser. No one in Discordia would ever be so crass as to admit knowing what anyone else is doing, especially someone from a different House. Each of their temples—Houses, they call them—is practically a law unto itself, though they pretend not to use that hideous word *law*. These wharves, for instance, are under the care of the House of the Rising Collapse. You can't see it from here, but that other big building looming upriver past the bridge is the House of the Rising Podge, a different administration altogether."

"Are they all so distinct?" asked Samareh. "I read something about the Discordian religion, but can't seem to make head or tail of it."

"Oh, don't let them hear you call it a religion!" said Culler. "They certainly wouldn't like that. There is no generally accepted exposition of their tenets, even among themselves. I have, however, made a certain study of this matter and I can offer what seems the most plausible explanation. Discordia originated more than fifteen hundred years ago, in the midst of a civilization quite different from our own. As new spiritual entities tend to do, it positioned itself in opposition to the dominant culture of its time, which was characterized by rational industrial order, obsessive programmatic planning and elaborate bureaucracy. Hence the mocking, mixed, disorderly and antinomian tone of the *Principia Discordia* and their other scriptures and poems."

"You seem well informed. Who was Malaclypse the Younger?"

"Who knows? A vagabond who dwelt long ago in sunny California, that land of Cockayne now lost beneath the waves. I have lived in many places and done many things, and conversed with doctors, miners, soldiers and farmers, reflecting on what wisdom they choose to share. I find the best information, in fact, comes from tavern keepers, though it is always gemstones in a slurry, you know. I would venture to say I know a thing or two, but the recondite details of the *Principia* are beyond me, as they are beyond most of these Discordians who learn the book by heart. May I go on?"

"Please," she said, shifting away from his hand, which had crept toward her on the stone.

"Well, in that ancient, highly ordered society of long ago, for reasons that are now obscure, many common activities such as agriculture, transport and the trades, natural philosophy, police work and so on were thought of as somehow separate from religion."

Samareh attempted to digest this. "How could that be? Everything is intrinsically part of religion. It is impossible to separate them."

"Spoken like a partizan of Holy Commerce! You may well wonder, but this is what those people believed. They used the word *secular* to signify all those common areas of life that everyone engages in: love, food, labor relations and the like, which therefore cannot be thought of as contained within religion."

"And what about prayer and sacrifice, which everyone engages in?"

Culler glowed with pleasure as he spoke. "Yes, a crux! But in those days the ancient scholars and academics refused to acknowledge the validity of such acts as prayer and sacrifice: the words themselves were dismissed as misnomers that actually referred to other kinds of behavior. But this discussion would carry us too far afield. Suffice it to say that the Discordians of that time despised the so-called secular world, with its rational administration and its rules. They saw it as a place of dead-hand conformity, of stultifying routine crushing out the novelty and creativity that make life worth living. They identified five demonic all-controlling powers: 'The Party for War On Evil' which suppressed human diversity; 'The Knights of the Five Sided Temple' who were the enforcers; 'The Hemlock Fellowship' which dominated education, and so on, all under a sort of evil demiurge or false creator whom the Discordians call Old Gray Face, or Nobodaddy. In resistance to this grim figure they worship lovely Eris the Goddess of Discord, who appears in various forms of ravishing beauty and sometimes of gruesome rage, and in whom they see the embodiment, rather blood-spattered of creation itself and the fountain of all exuberance, the young plant breaking from the frozen earth, the angel lifting the stone from the sepulcher of cosmic consciousness, etcetera."

"So they thought system and structure were evil? Such beliefs might complicate their own religious organization."

"No doubt," answered Culler. "But time changes all things. As ancient America fell into ruins, the Discordians, who for some reason had become numerous in this region, were obliged to develop their own organization and procedures—to become, in a sense, the local replacement for the old system they despised. The Discordians of our time actually have a well-functioning religious organization, but they avoid the name and conceal the fact under a clown mask and harlequin's tassels. Such is their way, and it works as well as any. I assume you came in through the South Gate. Did you see the uniformed soldiers tied up?"

"Yes. It looked strange."

"Strange or no, it's Discordian to the core. The bound soldiers in fancy uniforms represent the Knights of the Five-Sided Temple, incapacitated by glorious all-conquering Eris, who has symbolically thrown the gates wide open. But in the real world where we actually live, gates sometimes need to be guarded. Those ragged fellows carrying the guns were the on-duty guards, and pretty well trained, though pretending to be dancing scarecrows. Every three days they switch places with the tied-up men in a private ceremony that no one is allowed to view. Everything here is like that: formal honors given to Scandal-Strewing Eris even as the people go about their normal routines. Ludicrous, but it functions. Do you see what my men are unloading from that ship?"

"Dirty gray shards, it looks like. What are they?"

"Aluminum!" He relished her puzzled expression. "You've seldom heard of it, but it used to be quite the thing, in the old days. We dig it up in ruined towns and ancient rubbish heaps in the suburbs of Old Baltimore, haul it upriver and sell it to the House of the Rising Collapse, the most potent and mysterious of the Discordian factions."

"And what do they do with it?"

Culler shrugged. "Nothing that I know of. Aluminum has no value. What you see there is its corroded form. When melted it becomes white silvery metal, strangely light but too brittle to work, and too soft for regular use. Pots and bowls made of it soon crack and dent. It conducts electricity, but not as well as copper which is much easier to wire-draw. As a building material it is useless, nor is it good for tools. Even when made into decorative items or jewelry it soon turns that dull gray color, and nothing will polish it. It is a most characteristic product of those ancient days: useless but imperishable. No one knows why they made so much of it. It is sometimes derisively called 'American Silver.' The Rising Collapsers pay modestly for it, store it with care and I believe from time to time they melt it in a ceremony, but they never say what use they make of it—I've asked. My personal opinion is that they believe such pointless hoarding of a useless metal greatly honors their goddess, as a kind of homeopathic parody of the lost industrial culture that Discordia once rebelled against. They call this sort of work 'Immanentizing the Eschaton'—a philosophical conceit. Now dear Samareh, this rock on which we sit is beginning to feel rather hard, and the sky looks like it might be coming on to rain. While my men work, allow me to treat you to a light repast in a local tavern, that we may continue this diverting conversation."

"Perhaps not," said Samareh, once again avoiding his hand as she stood. "But I would like to see this warehouse where they keep the aluminum scrap, if you are going there later." It had occurred to her that such a place, heaped with bales of rubbish, might be used for concealing other things as well. Culler, after several more attempts to lure her which he at last gave up in frustration, said he would be taking his wagon there the following morning. "I doubt there is anything you would wish to see, but you may meet us there, if you must." He gave her directions to the Square. "Not before nine at the earliest; my men won't move until they've had their breakfast." Samareh left them and spent the rest of the afternoon in town making inquiries about the missing Yasion Flowell and his companion Deloit Valeho, but learned nothing of interest.

She did not wait for morning, but made her way through quiet empty streets an hour before dawn, to the Square of the Rising Collapse. The temple flanked one side of the square with a façade three hundred feet in length and seventy feet high. Its windowless, pilastered walls were of dressed stone, and a curious egg-shaped dome covered in green copper rose above the roof at one end, nearly doubling the height of the building. The metal sheeting had been partially removed from the dome's upper courses, leaving dark gaps near the top like lookout posts. Samareh saw no one, and finding no opening in the wall that faced the square, she began to go around. In the short wall farthest from the dome she found an open archway bearing the Hand of Eris above a double-leaf bronze gate that had been standing open so long that wide green stains ran from it across the stones. She walked through, and found to her puzzlement that the interior of the great structure was open to the sky, except at the end that supported the dome. The cyclopean outer walls were a false front for a warren of three-and-four story buildings of various ages and designs packed within, set at strange angles to each other with narrow, mazelike lanes and little stone-paved courtyards in between. She followed the widest lane, under flags and bunting, and soon came upon a double-door warehouse, also bearing the sign of the Hand. One of its sliding doors hung partly open.

Without unnecessary noise Samareh drew her pistol, a semi-automatic from the Commercial Arsenal at Albany, cocked it, engaged the safety and reholstered. She went to the edge of the door, peered in, saw no one and slipped inside. The room was large and filled to more than twice the height of a man with bales of gray aluminum scrap tightly bound with wire. The ceiling was a high arched vault. Cool pre-dawn light spilled in through the open door, illuminating the wall of bales. A faint muffled sound came from somewhere out of sight above, followed by the clink of something moving, and another voice.

The bales to the left were not stacked as steeply as the rest, so that someone might climb them to reach the top, but there would be no way to do it quietly. "Whoever is up there," Samarah called, "I'd like to speak with you." Silence; she was going to have to be more direct. In a few quick, clattering bounds she made her way to the top of the bales and stood, listening. The irregular upper surface of the stacked bales stretched away into shadow. She drew her gun and held it pointed down as she proceeded, stepping from bale to bale. Some of the stacks reached higher; there were many places where an attacker could lurk unseen. Each step produced its clanking, creaking share of noise. She stopped again, with a strong sense of someone near. "I am not here to hurt you, or Discordia. I am an agent of the Admirate of Commerce, following my own orders just as you, perhaps, are following yours. If you know of anything wrong that has happened here, or anyone in danger, please tell me, so that I can help."

"That's a fine speech," came a voice from the shadow of a heap of bales. "It'd feel more sympathetic if you weren't carrying that heater." A tall woman wearing a jacket, trousers and boots of brown leather, and a tight leather cap with the side flaps folded up, stepped into the faint light. She held one arm out, hand around the grip of a powerful wrist-mounted slingshot, pointed at Samareh. "Don't worry about the pistol, just keep your arm down, or I'll put a ball in your eye. You say you're from the Admirate. Who you after?"

"Two men, Yasion Flowell and Deloit Valeho, with a shipment of coffee."

The woman laughed a little. "I know what Admirate walking papers look like. Show me some." Samareh put her free hand into her jacket, took out her otterskin folder and held it up, open. The woman seemed to recognize it, and relaxed. "All right. Now toss your gun over."

"No. You either trust me or you don't. I'm inclined to trust you. I'll holster it." She released the hammer and slipped the piece inside.

The tall woman frowned, then shrugged and lowered her arm, relaxing the elastic sling. "You're a chilly one, Admirate, but I figure you're okay."

"Is there someone else up here? I heard voices, and a groan."

"Come over, I'll show you. My name's Marg. Marg Sunnalo of Overlook Mills." Samareh followed her to a depression in the scrap where a blanket had been spread out. On it lay a young man with short brown hair, his abdomen indifferently bandaged with strips of his torn shirt, sticky with congealing blood. His ragged breath was slow.

"You know him?" asked Marg.

"Yes, it's Valeho. How did this happen?" She knelt by him to probe the bandage. Deloit's jaw clenched; he tried to speak but failed.

"Crossbow bolt bounced off something and into his side, maybe six hours ago? It's not in too deep, but it's wedged against a rib and I didn't try to dig it out."

Samareh looked up. "Shot by who? A Discordian?"

Marg's face was brown and freckled, and coils of copper hair escaped from her cap. She looked bemused. "That wouldn't narrow it down much, would it? Discordia's not one thing, Admirate girl. You want to tell me your name, by the way?"

"Samareh LaTrobe. I didn't mean any offense. Do you know who did this?"

Marg gestured to the wound. "Crossbow. Heavy, serviceable and cheap, and you don't need much training to use one. That kind of weapon is carried by a lot of low-life characters. Mister Deering Culler's men, for example."

"Culler, of course. All that time he was giving me the eye, he must have been planning this. But people like him are always in the pay of someone else. Do you know who?"

"Nope. Someone over the mountains, mos' likely."

"Cleveland," said Deloit in a soft, wrecked voice. His eyes caught the faint light as he looked up, taking shallow breaths. "Cleveland party. North. Took shipment."

Samareh knelt and bent close to listen. "Why would Cleveland come this far to steal a load of coffee?"

"Not coff . . ." Deloit struggled for breath, and with a weak hand he gestured toward a small cloth-wrapped bundle nearby. Samareh took it up and opened it. Inside were several loose coffee beans, and the warhead of a rocket-propelled grenade.

"Now I see why they didn't want to take the northern route." Samareh turned to Marg. "Are you helping them?"

"Me? I ain't helping them, strict to say. Just saw an opportunity to escalate. That's what we do." At Samareh's puzzled expression she recited: "'Every action and circumstance must be escalated to its most perfect form—thence springs Chaos!' That's from the Principles, or from some other book like it. I overheard these two boys talking at the Plowman's Rest a few days back, about a shipment that had been yanked. It sounded like great game. From their description I figured it was Culler's men that took it, and I know they come here to sell their scrap. Last night I showed Deloit and Yaz how to get in here, figuring they'd scope the place and be back safe once they learned something. When they didn't show I came looking, and found this. He must have scrambled up here after they shot him, and they didn't stick around to finish the work. I'd just stanched the bleeding when you showed up."

Samareh stood up. "That shipment must have been arms for the Pittsburgh government, and the Cleveland-Youngstown faction had their man Culler and his people hanging around here, on the chance that something like that might come through. I met them yesterday. But if they got the weapons weeks ago, why didn't they run? Why wait until now?"

"Makes sense," said Marg. "Cleveland don't need weapons; they just want to keep 'em away from the Pitters. Culler wouldn't know how many shipments might come through, so he just stayed on, waiting. But when you showed up he knew the bird was cooked. Must have smoked you out for a professional the moment he saw you—I know I did. Then they come here last night to grab the load, and found the boys. By my life, the Goddess puts things to work in funny ways. The breeze of wisdom and the wind of insanity blow together."

"Maybe so," said Samareh as she leaned over Deloit again. "We're going to get you to a doctor. What happened to Yasion? Do they have him? Do they know who he is?"

Deloit, in spite of his pain, managed a crippled grimace. "Yasion gone over to Cleveland. Took the load. He's the one that shot me."

They carried him out of the warehouse in the blanket, Marg going first and Samareh staggering behind. They found a delivery wagon and asked the driver to take them to a hospital not far from the temple. The city was coming to life in the gathering day, but no one showed much interest in two women and a bleeding man. The attending doctor wore a coat of pale duff printed with red splatter marks like smeared blood, but Samareh noticed after a moment that these were part of the coat's design, and all the staff wore the same colors. The hospital looked meticulously clean and well-managed. The doctor studied Deloit's wound and asked, "Are you from the incline?"

"No," said Samareh. "Did something happen?"

"We just heard by the city telegraph. Four men raided the lower station of the Waggoners Gap incline. They shot the booking officer and the carriage commander with bolts like the one in this man's side, loaded the incline carriage and took off up the mountain. Discord is in high fettle this morning! From the look of your man, I expect he'll live. Come back later after I've extracted the bolt."

As they left the office, Samareh asked Marg, "Where is the incline?"

"The bottom end of it's about fifteen miles west of here, where the steep hills begin. It runs ten miles up the slope at an angle, cross the front of the ridge. We use it to reach the Pennsylvania canal on the other side, 'cause old Suskehana's blocked with cumber just north of here and it's all rapids from the bridge to Marysville. You won't catch those guys—they've already started up."

"Is there any way to stop the incline on its way up the mountain?"

"Not likely, if they don't throw the brake themselves. The carriage is counterweighted by a car full of lead and granite that runs on its own track beside the main one. They raise the counterweight car every night by a water mill, and as it comes down it raises the carriage. They only run one trip each day."

"Then I'm a day behind them, at least."

Marg stopped. The sun was up, the day was clear and the courtyard around them was alive with Discordians going about their business, dressed in eccentric styles and colors but otherwise looking much like people anywhere. "So what's the big deal with this load? A few hundred pounds of weapons isn't going to change the outcome of a war, is it?"

Samareh took the grenade head from her coat pocket. "This is a shaped charge, armor-piercing, probably better than anyone could make out here. But you're right; they're not enough to change the war. The problem is Yasion. He's a close relative of Lobard Gullen-Barange, an important person in the Holy Admirate. Whatever the Clevelanders have promised Yasion, whatever mistaken yearning caused him to do this crazy thing, it's certain they'll treat him as a hostage, which could be a disaster. I must do whatever I can."

"That's the spirit." Marg stood with her hands on her hips, thinking. Shadows from the nearby buildings fell dark across the rough stone beyond her, while the western wall glowed in warm light. A small fountain sprayed jets of crystal water that rose and fell, sparkling in the day. "I have to puzzle on this," she said. "The Goddess likes sudden reversals. That boy is acting like an ally of Discord."

Samareh watched her closely. "But you're thinking of doing something anyway. Another reversal?"

"Maybe. So, have you figured out what I do?"

"I haven't had time to think about it. You're wearing leather and carrying a light weapon. Some kind of messenger?"

"Yep. But what kind? You know the rubric of the Rising Collapse?"

"I can't say I do."

Marg chanted:

> *"The Breeze of Wisdom and the Wind of Insanity,*
> *The Breeze of Integrity and the Wind of Arrogance,*
> *The Breeze of Beauty and the Wind of Outrages,*
> *The Breeze of Love and the Wind of Bombast,*
> *The Breeze of Laughter and the Wind of Bull—"*

"I get it," Samareh said, cutting her off. "Breeze and wind. You're a glider pilot."

"That's right—and the best in the Suskehana Valley! Messages and small cargo carried from Baltimore to Bethlehem and points in between, in a day or less if the money be seen."

"And could another person count as small cargo, and are you good enough to put one down on a slow-moving target?"

"For the love, girl, I put down a drunk river pilot on a tugboat once, in a thunderstorm. If you're ready to fight, I'll take you to the battle. I've made up my mind. Goddess help me if I turn down this chance."

The glider was a bi-wing covered in brown canvas over a light, strong frame, with a kerosene-powered starter engine, space for Marg to lie flat at the controls, and below her another sling for cargo or a passenger. They launched from one of the open galleries that Samareh had seen earlier near the top of the Rising Collapse dome, where the machines of several glider pilots were stored. Marg got Samareh lashed in, spun the propeller to crank the starter engine, and then fairly ran the machine out through the opening, plunging a hundred feet before the wings caught the air and they rose, over the rooftops of 'Arrisburg. Samareh saw laundry on the line flash by, chimney pots and a couple having breakfast on a balcony, who raised their mugs in salute. She closed her eyes and forced her stomach back down. When she looked again, they were passing over the river. Soon open country rolled beneath.

Farms and fields passed below, stone-walls, oak coppices, and fields gray with stubble. Catching an updraft, they soared, and Marg cut the little engine. Soon the rugged first range of the Blue Mountains drew near, covered in forest, with gray rock outcrops along its crest. Further west the higher ridges loomed, rank upon rank lit hazy blue by the rising sun. The silence and the splendor of the view made Samareh wonder what it must be like not to care about life and death and responsibility, but just to live; perhaps that was part of what it meant to be a Discordian. An eagle passed below them, and almost as it came the thought faded. She was an officer of the Holy Admirate with work to do, and that was that.

The incline railroad lay at a shallow angle against the front of Blue Mountain, its course rising gently toward the rocky notch of Waggoners Gap. There were two lines of rails, one for the carriage and another for the counterweight, which was rolling down at the same slow rate that the carriage moved up. A braided steel cable ten miles long, an ancient treasure of great value and craftsmanship that had been spliced countless times, ran on rollers from the carriage up to the high station, around a great pulley wheel and back to the counterweight. As the glider neared the mountain Samareh caught sight of the carriage through the trees, a square timber platform twenty feet on a side, one third of it enclosed by a wooden structure painted red with large windows, for passengers and delicate cargo. The rest was empty flatbed, occupied only by Culler's wagon, which no doubt contained many bales marked "Product of Jamaica." The carriage was more than halfway up the slope; the counterweight well below it.

"You have the grenade?" Samareh called.

"Sure enough," shouted Marg over the wind, and patted the grenade in its pouch beside her, wrapped in cloth made sticky with raw paraffin.

"And you remember what to do?" They had installed a makeshift fuse.

"Goddess love you girl, I'm not six years old! You just leave your work to you and mine to me. You think I'm gonna pass up a chance to cause this much havoc, when the Admirate's taking the blame?"

Samareh decided to worry about that later. She said no more as they descended toward the track. Marg brought the glider in a few hundred feet below the carriage, then flew close above the rails as Samareh, one hand on the buckle of her harness and the other gripping her gun, waited to jump. At the last instant Marg pulled back and up, putting the glider into a near stall directly over the deck of the carriage. Samareh wrenched the buckle, fell ten feet to the deck and tumbled forward, rolling, as a crossbow bolt fired from the carriage house door whipped past her head. Craine stood there. Someone else inside fired through an open window at the glider, as Marg flipped sideways out of the stall and swooped away, low over the ground, heading back down the slope.

Samareh got behind a stack of boxes that braced the wagon, as another bolt ripped the wooden deck by her knee. She leaned around the crates and fired twice at Craine. He went down and she ran forward. The door slammed, and a window slid open. She fired, breaking glass. She reached the door. Finding it locked, she checked that the hinges opened inward and then kicked it, hard, beside the handle. A bolt from the nearby window nicked her arm and the door frame, the head whipping past her face as it spun away. She fired again. She kicked the door again.

On the third try the frame splintered and she tumbled into the room beyond, scrambling to put a wall at her back.

"Don't shoot!" shouted Culler, whether to her or his men it wasn't clear. He stood near the control end of the car with windows behind him, and trees and sky beyond. He held a small crank-set crossbow armed and cocked, pointed toward the back of Yasion Flowell who knelt before him, looking pale and seedy. Across the room one of Culler's men, Craine, lay moaning atop a smear of blood. The other one, Mark, stood holding the second crossbow, pointed at Samareh's chest.

"This is monstrously inconvenient!" Culler said in a harsh, aggravated voice. "What did you think to gain by such a stunt? Why are you being so infernally persistent?"

"What about you?" she replied, panting and wondering how much time Marg would need to plant the grenade on the cable. "Who are you doing this for, Culler? Whatever they are paying you isn't worth it; every agent in the Admirate will come for your head when they learn of this."

"And how do you imagine they'll learn?" Culler prodded Yasion, who was livid and silent, his slack face looking like it had been rubbed with cooking oil. "This young gentleman knows by now that he's more along the lines of baggage, rather than a paying customer."

"Whatever he is, he's not going with you to Cleveland."

Culler blinked but did not smile. "I see no reason not to kill you. Shoot her, Mark. She won't fire. She's got an obligation to protect this whelp."

Samareh turned to Mark, who stood unhappy with his drawn crossbow. "If you shoot me I will kill you, Mark. Do you think he would care? But if you help me there will be a big reward."

"Dunno what I think about this," Mark growled, his eyes shifting between Samareh, her gun and the face of Culler. "It's all gone bad since that stupid kid shot his friend."

"You don't need to think!" shouted Culler. "Do what I say!"

Before Mark could answer, the sound of a sharp, distant explosion rattled the windows. The carriage lurched to a halt and then began rolling back downhill, gaining speed. Culler barked a curse. "You witch! You've cut the cable!"

"With a grenade," she said.

"The brake!" Culler screamed, lunging for the controls. "There must be a brake lever . . ."

Mark fired his crossbow, perhaps not certain whether he wished to hit Samareh or Culler. The bolt missed both, sticking in the back of a chair near Culler's hand. Culler shouted more curses and fired his own weapon. The bolt hit Mark in the stomach and he fell, moaning. Then Samareh shot Culler. He roared and fell sobbing. "This was your plan? This was your stupid, stinking . . ." The carriage shook, its speed increasing every moment.

"Call it a Discordian plan." Samareh ran for the brake lever. In truth, she had not had much idea what she would do when Marg blasted the cable. The object had been to stop the carriage; everything else depended on circumstance. She threw her weight against the lever, but either some other mechanism was involved, or the carriage was already moving too fast for it to hold. A metallic scream sounded from below, but the speed only increased. She went to Yasion, still kneeling sickly and distraught, and dragged him to his feet. "If we're going to jump off of this thing we should go now, before we're rolling any faster. Come!"

As she pushed Yasion out the door, something struck her arm with such force that it wrenched her around and knocked her down. Culler, still lying on the floor, had recovered enough strength to reload. His face was hideous. Samareh looked blankly at the small four-flange head of the bolt, and an inch of shaft, covered in her blood and sticking through her forearm halfway between elbow and hand. The pain was extraordinary.

She crawled out of the cabin onto the open deck. The forest slid past at a ridiculous rate. Yasion was nowhere to be seen; perhaps he had already leaped. Wind whipped her hair as the carriage rocked from side to side, dislodging the wagon. It tumbled over the edge and was gone. The rocking became more violent. She wondered whether the carriage would derail and kill her before she reached the bottom of the hill and died there. In her dazed condition the problem seemed insoluble and at the same time oddly impersonal.

A brown biplane glider appeared in her view at eye level, somehow keeping its place between the rushing trees and the tottering carriage. A woman in brown leather was shouting at her. She went forward, gripping the harness and struts so that she was lifted, crazily, into the air. In that moment they passed through an open place clear of trees, and she saw sunlight on the frame of the glider: bright metal streaked with pale oxide. *American Silver*, she thought, and they crashed.

Samareh rolled on grass and came to rest against a deadfall and some rocks, realizing after a few hard breaths that her body was not going to do her the favor of blacking out. The bolt still protruded from her ruined arm, blood trickling weakly down its shaft. Silence fell. A wind sighed in the trees. Then she heard Marg somewhere nearby on the ground weakly laughing, and singing:

"Hail Eris, rub-a-dub dub!
Hail O Goddess, Davak-Tav-Yaska!
Hail, hell, I think my wrist's a-busted. Are you alive, Admirate girl?"

"I am," Samareh croaked. "And it hurts."
"It does, it does! Hail rub-a-dub dub!"

THE LAST KNUT OF LINSEY ISLAND

BY TONY F. WHELKS

Karel was sculling his coracle from buoy to buoy in the mussel beds when the Fowkers came. He was oblivious to their approach in the sea fog, his attention on the half-dozen ropes encrusted with blue-black shells that nestled between his feet. It was a good haul, more than enough for the Portioners' tithe, and he would soon be done for the day, once the slack tide turned to carry him back to the shore. He laid the paddle across his lap and stretched out the harvester over the side. The precious iron hook caught first time and Karel levered the shaft slowly, careful not to capsize the coracle as he heaved against the weight.

The end of the rope lifted over the rim, water dripping like pearls back into the glassy sea, and he let the drips cease before flicking the catch inboard.

Then he saw it.

A carved figurehead loomed from the mist as the Fowker ship glided in, barely rippling the water at its bow. Karel fumbled in panic as he put the paddle into the water and frantically turned the blade. His heart beat like a giant drum as he strove to evade the raiders, but for all its manoeuvrability, the coracle was not a swift craft. He was barely under way before he heard a shout behind him. The Fowkers had spotted him, and a score of oars splashed into the water and bit deep. Karel could hear the the foreign coxswain as he called the rowers' beat. They were gaining on him, and still the shore was shrouded in mist. Dodging through the buoys where his earlier harvesting had cleared a path, he had one hope of escape.

The clatter of wood on wood brought a brief smile to his face, and the coxswain's cursing confirmed his hopes. The deep-biting oars of the Fowkers were battering at buoys and snagging the mussel-ropes. He turned his paddle in elegant figure of eight strokes, but knew he could only make slow headway as the raiders cleared their oars of the fouling ropes. "Hup, hup, hup," he heard once more, a faster beat, and Karel knew the coxswain had ordered shallow strokes, barely scraping the limpid surface.

Relief surged through him as he spied a darker mass ahead. Surely he must be reaching the mud flats? He shouted a warning, "Fowkers! Fowkers!" If only he could alert the villagers and the Portioner's men, bring them to the shore, perhaps, perhaps. . . .

His hopes were dashed, though. When the dark mass resolved through the mist, Karel saw a second ship ahead. He was trapped between two raiders, his flight over.

The crowd of women swarmed around the Portioners' Hall, banging their pots and pans together, their angry yells all but drowned in the din of the clanging metalware. Inside, the Portion Council tried to conduct their deliberations, but the noise was a distraction if not a complete impediment.

"What do they want?" snarled Masterportioner Albret, although he knew the answer well enough. "What do they expect?"

"They want to go home, m'lud," replied Jax, unnecessarily. Jax was the Council Clerk, a diffident young man more at ease recording the deeds and decisions of others than putting forth his own thoughts. He even looked like a reed, trembling and wind blown, yet somehow sure-footed in the shifting tides of Council affairs.

"I know that, you fool! We all know that. And we all know what will happen if they do, and they like that even less."

Albret glowered around the table. It was stacked with hand-drawn maps, lists of names and places, harvest tallies and tithing receipts. Not one of the Councillors would meet his gaze, not that he could blame them. Stuck between the devil and the deep blue sea, whatever they decided would be wrong. The Portioning always upset someone. Sometimes it upset everyone, Albret included.

A heavy set man in his early fifties, Albret was young for a Masterportioner, his black hair and beard barely speckled with grey. The Council had needed a firm hand at the helm following his predecessor's untimely and messy demise. He had been weak, irresolute in the face of the crisis brought about by the Red Sky Winter. Now, nearly two decades on, the effects of that three year spell of cold and dark were still reverberating around Linsey Island. The Portioning was always a cruel calculation, and an oversized cohort of youths due to reach maturity loomed like a tidal wave on the horizon. It was never easy to redivide the holdings, assign families to new villages. That's why the Council was only ever drawn from the Brother and Sister Houses, men and women with no children of their own to favour.

Albret banged his meaty fist to the table. "A curse on this infernal racket! Call the militia. I want the streets cleared. And bring that madwife Meryn in here. She's the ringleader. Let's see if we can talk some sense into her stubborn head."

The council chamber was quiet by the time the guards returned with Meryn, a midwife despite the common slur uttered by Albret earlier. Like the turning tide, Albret showed a gentler face to the young woman standing before him.

"Please be seated, goodwife, and explain what you hope to achieve with all this noise and fury," he said, waving his left hand in airy circles.

"I don't believe you don't know," countered Meryn, still bristling at the rough treatment meted out by the militia.

"Humour us. Perhaps we have misjudged you with our assumptions."

Meryn tried not to roll her eyes at this. "Maybe you have; maybe you have misjudged us with this ridiculous policy. The women simply want to go back home. The hostels and lodges are crowded, the children are going spare, and we can all see that the tasks you've allotted are nothing but makework when we have real work going undone back in our own villages. Tell us the truth. Whatever reason you have for bringing us here, it is not what you told us."

"Really? And what do you imagine our reasoning was?" He turned an amused smile around the group of twenty men and women who constituted the Portion Council. His condescension was clear in his expression. *See what foolish children we must govern,* it seemed to say.

"I think that's for the Council to explain. I wouldn't want to misjudge you with assumptions," the midwife retorted.

Albret heaved a sigh. "Very well. I'm sure you are a devout woman, but you are not privy to the census returns, are you? Soon the Winterborn will be coming of age, and you have no idea how numerous they are. We have placed great faith in the midwives and herbwives, but still families grow. If only your women could breed land the way they breed babies!"

"I'm sure even a Brother knows the facts, my lord. The women don't do it alone."

"That's why they have been separated from their menfolk," said Albret, exasperation in his voice. "Each Parish takes its turn, year and year about. We know it's not popular, but the figures show it was working, until you whistled up this storm! What would you have us do? Go back to culling the first-born? Pick another war with the Umbran Isles so your sons can be slaughtered? Sell your daughters to the slavers? What sacrifice do you propose?"

Meryn glanced at the silent, robed figure seated beside Albret. "Do your duty to the Gods, perhaps? Until we atone for our forefathers' sin, the waves will keep eating away our land. Find a worthy Knut, one who can fulfill the prophecy."

When Karel regained consciousness the throbbing of his head made him wince. The sky was bright, too bright now the fog had burnt away, and he scrunched his eyes tight to ease the pain. His hands were bound behind him, rough hemp cutting into his wrists. Venturing a peek, he peered through slitted eyelids to find a hulking giant of a Fowker standing guard over him. Looking around he could see another four of the sleek, shallow-draughted raiding ships alongside the one on which he was held captive. Five ships; a hundred men at least, he reckoned. The village wouldn't stand a chance, whether or not they had heard his warning shout. Even the Portioner's squadron, in the village conducting their tithing rounds, would be hard-pressed by such a band.

He oriented himself and glanced ashore. There were bodies at the water's edge, and bile rose in his throat. Further along, a dejected looking group of captives were surrounded by spear-wielding Fowkers, and in the distance a plume of smoke roiled, thick and dirty from burning thatch. Racks of sun-dried jellyfish glowed softly in the morning sun, like a ghostly shieldwall, ephemeral and useless.

Karel watched on, impotent as the raiders prodded the captives to their feet, and marched them through the shallows towards the waiting boats, five or six to each one. They were all young, like Karel. When they were brought on board, Jenna, one of his friends from the village, was thrust down beside him on the rough bench.

"What happened?" he whispered.

"What do you think?" the girl hissed back.

"Anyone get away in time?"

"No."

An ice cold ball of dread settled in his stomach, and he gulped down a wave of nausea.

"My parents?" he hissed.

"I'm sorry, Karel. Mine too. All the old people."

"Bastards!"

One of the Fowkers stepped towards Karel and levelled a spear-tip to his throat. "No talking, Yellowbelly," he growled.

"Fowk off!"

"Funny. You're a funny boy, I've never heard that one before." The Fowker forced a guttural laugh and made to turn away, then swung back, landing a booted foot into Karel's stomach. Karel heaved a dry retch and doubled over, trying to catch his rasping breath. By the time he recovered, all but one of the ships had been pushed out, and only a handful of the raiders remained ashore, waiting for who knows what.

Karel's spirits lifted then, as he caught the faint drumming of hooves carried on the breeze. A group of riders crested the hill beyond the village, and he could just make out the grey robes of Jon, the Portioner for the Parish of San Peterpoll, at the head of his bodyguard. The riders bore down on the group of Fowkers by the shore. Karel expected the men on foot to turn tail and run for the boats, but they stood their ground as the cavalrymen approached. He held his breath, waiting for the riders to couch their spears and spur their horses for the charge, but the charge never came. Instead, Portioner Jon pulled up in front of the raiders, and spoke briefly to their leader, who tossed up what looked like a leather purse. The Portioner caught the bundle and tucked it into his saddlebag before wheeling around and leading his troop away at a gentle trot.

Albret the Masterportioner let the shock show on his face. "Meryn," he rumbled, "I want you to think very carefully before you say any more." The Council members shifted uneasily in their seats, an undercurrent of tension sharpening their features and their attention. This was uncomfortably close to heresy, all the more uncomfortable for having been uttered in the very presence of the aged Knut herself.

"Are you denying the Knut," continued Albret, "or making a formal challenge?"

Caught in the dilemma, Meryn's faced paled. "I, I . . ." she stammered. "Forgive me, I spoke hastily."

"Indeed. But you spoke nonetheless. The words are out, and it's too late to swallow them now."

Meryn stood rooted to the spot, her mind feverishly running over the choice suddenly before her. She had overstepped the mark, she knew, changed the whole course of her life with an unguarded comment. The punishment for heresy was clear, yet she had had no intention of challenging the Knut, either.

She was no heretic. She believed. She believed the Old Words, she believed that one day a Knut would arise to turn back the tides and end this time of loss and suffering and deprivation. True, she didn't believe that the shrivelled husk sat before her was the one, any more than the long line of failed Knuts before her. But neither did Meryn believe that she herself had any claim over the power of the waves. She didn't believe the time was yet come. To deny the Knut was heresy—it was to say the time would never come. Meryn was no heretic, and so she spoke at last.

"I challenge the Knut," she conceded, already beginning to mourn the life she was to lose, one way or another.

Karel tried to keep his bearings by the sun that glared mercilessly over the quiet sea. To his surprise, he realised that the small fleet of raiders had not turned south back towards the Fowker Islands, but was heading northwards instead. His mind's eye kept replaying the scene of the Portioner catching the bag of silver, and inwardly he seethed at the betrayal. He and the other captives had been sold, their families slaughtered, and here they were, being shipped away to the north. Maybe to the

Umbran Isles, though by now they should have been close inshore.

No, he thought, not Umbra. They had cleared the northern tip of the Serpent's Back and with it all hope of rescue by the Linsey fleet stationed on that long, thin spit of land to police the trade lanes. They were heading into the wide expanse of York Sound, and if they weren't bound for Umbra, then their destination could only be one of the ports on the mainland. One of the slave states. It made sense, he mused. That's why the Fowkers had only taken the youngest. That he would never return to Linsey and expose the treachery of Portioner Jon only stoked Karel's rage and deepened the misery of this unwanted journey.

He could do nothing but bide his time and nurse his resentment.

Meryn's challenge against the Knut took precedence over all other business for the Council. Pressing as the annual Portioning was, it could not proceed until the challenge had been tested and resolved. It was a complication he could well have done without, but Albret adjourned the convocation overnight and called his closest advisers into his chamber.

"How in blazes do we do this?" he shouted, as soon as the door was shut. "We've not had a challenge for generations!" The practice had fallen into disuse since the Knut's temporal power had been curtailed. Now only the religious aspects of the position remained.

"If I may," Jax said. "I believe the ritual is outlined in the Annals."

"Thank the Gods. Find it and bring it to me."

"Of course."

Sarra, the elderly Knut, eased herself into a padded wooden chair. "Well!" she exclaimed, a peevish tone to her thin voice. The challenge to her authority, her ability, had shaken the old woman. "What does that impudent child know of anything? She doesn't know the rituals, the pains I go to at every spring and neap. How dare she blame me?"

"The breeders do not understand the battle must be fought on two fronts. Oh, they want their children and their families, but they don't want the small Portions that go with that," growled Albret.

"Her challenge will fail. It must," insisted Sarra.

Albret slumped heavily into a chair at the head of his table, and with a gesture indicated that the others should also be seated. "We shall see what the Annals have to say on the matter," he said. "Meanwhile, what do we know about goodwife Meryn? Sister Anya, I believe she's a northerner?"

The tall blonde-haired woman leaned forward in her chair. "That's true, Masterportioner, from San Peterpoll, my own parish. I know the family. Her father and brother are fishermen, and her mother is a midwife, too. They're respectable people, no trouble to the Sister House at all and the two men take their turns on the patrol ships. So far as I know they pay their tithes on time, but you'd need to check that with the Brother House. They cast the nets in our parish."

"But it's not your parish on work rotation though, Anya, so why is she here?"

"No, with her mother being midwife there, Meryn was assigned to Allsan parish once she'd finished her apprenticeship, and it's those women who are here in Westport now."

"Causing all the trouble," observed Albret.

The Fowkers rowed in shifts throughout the night, their way lit by the fat waxing moon. Karel had been more than ready for the small ration of saltfish and stale water the Fowkers had issued to their captives. His bonds had been released long enough for him to eat, but with his guard's spear prodding him in the back he knew it was useless to even attempt anything. All too soon, his meagre meal was finished and his hands bound once more and the damp rope continued to chafe at his sore wrists. He had thought sleep would be impossible, but exhaustion, inadequate food and his earlier concussion weighed heavily, the rolling of the ship and the rhythmic beat of the oars lulled his senses, and he nodded off a few times, jerking awake in confusion each time his head lolled on to his chest.

Dawn broke over the dark waters of York Sound, and the grey smear of a distant shore loomed ahead. The little flotilla's course had changed overnight, the rising sun to their rear telling Karel that they now bore due west. The long sleek ships skimmed across the lazy waves, steering towards the twin promontories guarding a broad, sheltered bay. Laden merchant ships filed out of the harbour mouth, low and sluggish in the water, under the vigilant watch of an armed patrol ship backing water against the tide. A fast skiff darted out from behind the fighting vessel and intercepted the Fowkers' lead ship. A few words were exchanged, too distant for Karel to hear, but the skiff's crew tossed a pennant across, a courtesy flag which the Fowkers hoisted immediately.

The early morning light illuminated a mass of buildings clustered along either shore, but they were not of the wood and thatch construction Karel had known all his life. These looked like pale stone, whitish grey, or baked clay, glowing in their sunrise hues. The scale of the settlement was beyond any Karel had known back on Linsey Island, even though he could see much that seemed in ruins. Even Eastport and Westport were mere villages compared to this expanse.

A long wharf lined the waterfront, and the Fowker crewmen prepared to land. Oarsmen fore and aft skillfully brought the hulls into alignment and shipped oars as the gliding craft covered the final stretch of water. Ropes were thrown ashore and secured by desultory wharfmen working under the close but languid scrutiny of a posse of armed men.

The Fowkers' leader leapt ashore to greet a richly-dressed official, whilst one of his comrades started bellowing orders.

"Right, you Yellowbellies! Stand up and get moving!"

Karel and his fellow captives stumbled to their feet, struggling to balance in the bobbing ship with their hands tied. The crude gangplank was narrow and none too stable, but the prisoners shuffled along it one by one. Karel heard the Fowker chief laughing with the costumed panjandrum ahead, and another surge of fury at Portioner Jon's betrayal washed through him. He clenched his bound fists impotently, then a Fowker's heavy boot found his backside and propelled him forward on to the wharf. His dry lips were cracking with thirst, and the half-digested remains of the saltfish stirred his stomach uncomfortably.

Looking around him, Karel could see the wharfmen were hobbled, though their hands were free to work. Their clothing was rough, little better than sacking, whilst the guards wore leather breast-plates over long linen tunics and breeches not unlike his own, except for the colours. The soldiers' linens were dyed a strong blue, whereas his own were undyed, and after the rough voyage they were no longer particularly clean, stained by the foul splashes from the Fowkers' bilge and crusted over with dried salt-spray. He looked as he felt, a weather-beaten and downcast drudge, and his companions looked no better. The cluster of captured villagers milled around on the wharf, bewildered. Behind them the Fowker crewmen wielded their spears, and ahead, the blue-clad soldiers were being roused to action by the peacock of an official.

"Welcome to the Meerat of Braffur," he sneered. To Karel's ears, his accent sounded as clipped as the Fowkers' was slurred, with short vowels and hard consonants. "I trust your stay with us will be short and profitable. It will also be comfortable, if your behaviour is acceptable. Escape is not only unwise, but impossible." The official nodded to the guards, who advanced towards the captives, their vicious-looking polearms held ready, and proceeded to separate the young men and boys from the women and girls. They led the females away first, through a heavy gate set into a tall, wooden stockade. As they passed, the official marked off their numbers on a tally board.

"Ik, do, teen, cha . . ." he counted to himself, then grunted in satisfaction as the last girl entered and the gate closed behind her.

Karel felt panic rising within him, but he was still tightly bound, and the soldiers outnumbered the remaining villagers. The gateway before him marked the end of all hope.

‡‡‡

By the time Jax returned from the archives bearing the battered old volume of the Annals of Linsey, Albret's patience was worn even thinner than its usual diaphanous state. "I've found what we need, Masterportioner," the clerk gasped, somewhat breathless from scurrying through the hallways and corridors of the Portion Hall.

"Well? What is it, man? What must we do?" Albret snapped.

Jax, face flushed with the exertion, lay the thick, leather-bound book on the Masterportioner's table, but kept a hand firmly on its front cover as though holding it closed to prevent any secrets escaping unbidden. "A quick word first," he said, and beckoned to Albret to come closer. The two huddled together, heads bent towards one another, murmuring quietly.

"I see," said Albret, and he turned to the Knut, still seated in the corner of the room. "I'm sorry, Sarra, but I must ask you to leave. It seems the Knut is forbidden any foreknowledge of the . . . ritual," he amended, not wishing to use the word he first conceived, *trial.*

"Preposterous!" the elderly woman declared. "Ritual is the domain of the Knut! I don't see—"

"Nor can you see, Knut," Albret interrupted. "It is written, and we are bound. I'm sure you of all people understand that ritual must be followed to the letter? To offend the Gods so would only compound our forefathers' sin. A challenge has been raised, however unwisely, and we must see it through. It is written."

Visibly angered by this rebuttal, Sarra slowly rose from her seat, and left the chamber without another word. Once the door closed behind the Knut, and her shuffling footsteps had receded, Jax addressed the remaining councillors, explaining the ritual as laid out in the ancient text. Even Albret was stunned into silence.

"So, explain that again, Meryn. They only bring us here to stop us tupping?" Hilda was incredulous.

"So says the Masterportioner," the midwife replied.

"He don't know my husband," Hilda chuckled. "Give him a pot of ale and a full pipe, that's all it takes. No interest for days."

Meryn allowed herself a brief smile. She had been brooding about the business of the Knut and her challenge. She really hadn't meant to do that, but, well, she often spoke before thinking, a fault she readily admitted. Chatting with Hilda always cheered her up and it was helping now as they sat together in the hostel. "Confined to barracks," as the militia officer had put it.

"You know, Hilda, I could give you something to pep him up a bit."

"I'd rather have a barrel of ale," the older woman retorted, and they both laughed. "Anyway, I've already had three, and that's been enough trouble."

"Lucky your eldest joined the Brotherhood," said Meryn.

"Well, there was never any doubt about that. You could always tell, even when he was a nipper. Anyway, the other two were Winterborn, and I'm not the best or worst on that score." That was true enough. The Knut's edicts placed heavy tithes on children, although the demands were eased if any took the vow and joined a Brother or Sister House.

"I barely remember the Red Sky Winter," Meryn admitted. "I was very young."

"Hungry times, they were," Hilda recalled. "A lot of the old folk didn't make it. The summers were so short, we barely got the crops in. Thank the Gods for the fishing, though you soon got sick of fish soup, I can tell you."

"Fish soup always reminds me of my childhood. That, and my mother always being so busy."

"She would have been, yes. Not many ways to keep warm, and the herbs were in short supply, too. Couple more years and all the Winterborn will be looking for their own holdings. The Portioners will have their work cut out, then, believe you me."

"Things can change in a year or two," Meryn replied, the laughter draining away. "There may be a new Knut by then," she added, in a near whisper.

Hilda looked up sharply. "What have you heard? Is the old bat ill? Do tell!"

Shadows still hung over the streets of Westport as the rider clattered into town, his horse foaming and sweating beneath him. The gates had only just been opened when he cantered through and bore down on the Portion Hall at a speed that would have been dangerous any later in the day. The streets were mostly empty but for tired night watchmen and a few early risers heading towards dairy or bakery.

The rider was already dismounting as his horse skittered to a halt in the Hall's courtyard, and he was running towards the entrance, satchel in hand, even before the bleary-eyed groom had grasped the dangling reins.

"Urgent message for the Masterportioner!" His shouting was enough to wake the town, let alone the doorman.

Albret preferred his news and dispatches to arrive after breakfast rather than before, and an urgent rider always heralded an ill-fated day. He held his hand out to the messenger. "Give me the bad news, then," he sighed. "No one rides like that to announce a record harvest."

Plucking at the straps which sealed the satchel, Albret flipped it open and pulled out the single hand-written note within. "Oh, by the Gods!" he exclaimed. "Whatever next?"

Jax appeared unannounced at the door to the chamber. "Bad news, m'lud?"

Albret just shook his head in dismay and passed the note over to the clerk to read for himself. As he read, Jax's face blanched, and before he could react further a small crowd had gathered, drawn by the messenger's commotion. He looked up and passed the note to the next person, Sarra, the Knut.

"Thank you, but please tell me," she replied, declining to take the scrap from his hand. In his shock, Jax had forgotten the Knut could not read. Although she had never married, neither had she entered a Sister House, and had consequently never been taught her letters.

It was Albret who took charge and relayed the news to the growing crowd. "Fowkers have raided San Peterpoll. There are no survivors. It appears they struck just before the tithing party arrived. Brother Jon is overseeing the burials."

"Gods, no!" cried Anya. "They can't all be dead, surely? Forgive me, I must return to the Sister House, there must be so much to do!"

Albret, with an unaccustomed tenderness, took Anya's hand and said gently, "There are no survivors in the village, but the Houses weren't attacked. They can fend for themselves; your place is here."

Pinch-faced, the Knut interjected, "It's that woman's fault! The Gods have taken offence at her challenge and now they punish us. It's her village they destroyed!"

"If you could read, you would realize the raid happened before the challenge," Jax snapped.

Albret cast a reproving glance at the clerk, but said nothing. The younger man's face flushed, but whether from anger or shame, Albret would rather not know. But there was something he did want to know. How had the Fowker ships evaded the patrols of the Linsey fleet?

Karel seethed under the gaze of the overseer, and for a while refused to answer the question. He was one of the dozen male captives kneeling in a line, hands bound behind them.

"Again. What is your occupation?"

Karel looked down, studied the sand between his knees, determined not to comply. There were footsteps behind him, and he felt the sharp point of a pole axe against the base of his skull.

"One last time, slave. Tell me your occupation, or I shall have to record you as spoilage."

"Fisherman," he admitted finally. Tempted as he had been to let the guard kill him there and then, Karel's courage failed him.

"Another one," sighed the overseer, before moving on to the boy kneeling beside Karel. "Now this one looks too young. I'll put you down for the pleasure house, I think."

"He's a fisherman, too," growled Karel. He understood the implications of what the overseer had said, even if the boy hadn't, and he suddenly realized the fate that most probably awaited the young women in the adjoining pen. He thought of Jenna. Maybe it was the desperate situation they were now in, maybe it was the warmth they had shared on the cold journey across the York Sound, but the thought of never seeing her again filled him with a dread that drowned out his fears for his own fate.

The overseer looked back at Karel. "Now he's found his tongue, it seems he can't leave it alone. Use it again without permission, and I'll have it cut out, do you understand me, slave?" Karel nodded, cowed, but counted it as a small victory when the overseer said "Fisherman" once more as he marked his tally and continued along the line.

Reaching the end of the line of captives, the overseer turned at last to the waiting Fowker chieftain, who was barely concealing his impatience with the procedure. The overseer spoke a number. The Fowker spat on the ground, clearly unimpressed.

"What can I say?" the overseer replied, giving a slight shrug. "You raid a fishing village, you get fishermen. You probably killed the valuable ones. A good blacksmith would be worth more than this lot together. These will go for rowers, and they're not even a full crew."

"I can take them to the Middle Lands instead," countered the Fowker.

The overseer smiled a smug smile. "You could try."

"Is that a threat?" The chieftain bristled. He surveyed the soldiers arrayed behind the captives, then the small body of unarmed men he had been allowed to bring ashore.

"Not at all. Friendly advice, that's all. Just imagine if word got out to the Linsey outpost on the Serpent's Back. They would be on you before you reach the Knotty Shore. All that extra rowing before you can pay off your crews, too. You won't get a better price; that's why you came here in the first place."

The chieftain spat once more, but this time into the palm of his hand, which he extended to the overseer. "You drive a hard bargain, but my men will eat well enough from it."

A thin line of militiamen held back the milling crowd that lined the square outside the Portion Hall. At the top of the steps, Masterportioner Albret was presiding over the formalities, the Councillors standing in a line behind him. The summer sun was bright, and Albret, dressed in his heavy formal robes and weighed down by duty, was not alone in feeling the oppressive heat. He held up his right hand to signal the beginning of proceedings, and the murmur of the crowd subsided as everyone strained to hear.

"People of Linsey," he intoned, "today we beg again the forgiveness of the Gods. We beg our release from the sins of our forebears. For it was written that seven times seven generations must atone for those sins before a Knut would arise to turn back the tides. Our Knuts have prayed and performed the rituals ever since, and all have been defeated by the waves. Today, Goodwife Meryn of San Peterpoll has challenged our Beloved Knut Sarra to prove her title and overturn the curse that still lies upon us. Fellow believers, join us now in prayer to lend Sarra the strength to meet this challenge and deliver us from our lamentations."

The gathered townsfolk bowed their heads and the hubbub subsided to a murmur of whispered recitation interspersed with the shushing of children, finally settling to a silence barely scratched by the rustle of genuflection.

Robed in white, Sarra was kneeling in the centre of the square, unaware of the trials that lay before her, shielded by the secrecy ordained in the Annals. After a suitably respectful period of silence, Albret spoke once more.

"Sarra, Beloved Knut, go now with the prayers of the people. May the Gods look favourably upon us and accept our atonement this day."

The procession set off from the square, the Knut escorted by half a dozen of the Portioners and a small ceremonial guard drawn from the militia. Crowds lined the streets down towards the harbour where a small ship waited to carry the party across to the Pup of Linsey, the small, sacred islet which stood proud of Linsey's south coast. The crowd were mostly silent, but a few called out blessings to cheer on the Knut. Sarra's face was drawn and pale, the effect heightened by the whiteness of the robe she wore. Those who knew her well thought she had aged a decade overnight, so deep were the worry lines as she walked to her uncertain fate. As Masterportioner, it had fallen on Albret to oversee the challenge and his own expression was grim despite his efforts to hold a cold face. The whole business of the Portioning was on hold, and the complications were mounting, as if there hadn't been enough to begin with. He could neither afford the time away from the Council chamber, nor deputize this ritual challenge. It was his painful duty to officiate. It was written.

Once the Fowkers had been paid off for their human cargo, their ships departed and the villagers were left alone with the slave traders. The transformation from prisoner to slave was marked by the exchange of wrist bindings for leg irons. Towards sunset their guards distributed a rough meal of unfamiliar flat bread with pitchers of water, and although bland, the meal was ample and more satisfying than the Fowkers' saltfish. Once they had eaten, they were led away to cells for the night. Overwhelmed with exhaustion, Karel was asleep atop the sack-cloth covered straw almost before the cell door was locked behind him. The morning came all too soon.

Jarred awake by the rattle of keys in the lock and the crash of the door being pushed open, Karel found himself instantly alert. The guard tossed another of the flat loaves towards him, and Karel scrabbled to catch it before it bounced to the grimy floor.

"Eat quickly. You're going to market," the guard said over his shoulder before moving to the next cell.

Back in the outdoor enclosure where they had been sold by the Fowkers, Karel and his fellow villagers found themselves as quickly sold to the fat ship owner who had sneeringly examined them. Despite his haggling, the amount of coin that changed hands was far larger than that which the Fowker chieftain had grudgingly accepted the day before. The perfumed slave trader had wrung his hands most apologetically whilst explaining how the fishermen were in such great demand for oarsmen, and how many competing ship owners had been sidelined in favour of his valued client.

Karel's sense of bitterness deepened. He could barely fathom the numbers, but it left a sour taste when he realised that more coin had changed hands for his life in these few days than he had ever hoped to earn for himself. Whatever it took, he vowed, Portioner Jon's treachery would be exposed. All he had to do was escape his bonds and somehow find his way home to Linsey. The hardest task, though, would be to find someone who would even listen to a poor fisherman.

Sarra's eyes widened as she saw the Knut's throne. It was little more than a block of carved stone in the rocky cove on the southern tip of the Pup, exactly where the Annals had described. When the ship had been beached on the shingle there had been no mistaking the throne as it lowered over the sloping beach where it met the cliffs. The tide now was slack, but the banded darkness staining the lower levels of the rock face gave an ominous foreboding of the ritual she was to endure.

The strand was steep and the shingle rolled and shifted underfoot, dragging down even the younger and more sprightly members of the party. The throne sat slightly askew, as though it had settled since its previous use decades ago.

Albret took the lead as the party clambered up the treacherous slope, Anya and another Councillor assisting Sarra behind him. At the top, the elderly Knut was guided into the throne's cold, stone seat. She had to be lifted into place, and her legs dangled over the ledge, her bare feet clear of the stones below. Her features were calm, an impassive expression that only broke once, when the clasps were attached over her wrists, binding them irrevocably to the throne's arms.

Albret placed a reassuring hand upon Sarra's shoulder, the waspish Knut he had known for years now lost behind the vacant stare of a doomed old woman. "Drive back the waves, Sarra. You are the Knut, you know the rituals and the sacred words.

We must leave you now, but we will all be praying for you. Take strength from that. Offer up our atonement, and Gods willing we shall bring you home at the next low tide."

Turning quickly to avoid the tears welling in her eyes, he led the party back to the ship already beginning to lift on the rising tide. As the ship sailed from view across the placid sea, salt water trickled down Sarra's face, eager for the coming re-union with the elemental force rising to welcome it back to the fold.

Jax was enjoying the quietness of the Council Hall. It was rare for him to have the corridors and chambers to himself, but with the Challenge under way, the remaining Councillors were out of the way and Jax's fastidiousness was eating at him. With the Portioning on hold, papers and scrolls lay scattered about the large table in the Masterportioner's chamber, and the untidiness of it all had been a constant irritant. Quietly humming to himself, Jax set about re-organising the records, Parish by Parish, so the maps and lists and tithing returns were all collated properly. He liked things neat, and there was one pile of papers that screamed out at him because of the the work that would now have to be scratched out and begun again from fresh. San Peterpoll.

It bothered him that his compassion for the slain should be sullied by his jubilation over the vacant holdings that were now available for Portioning. Perhaps some of the tougher decisions the Council had been forced to make so far might be rethought. With luck, the Council may be able to uncork some of the pressure building up with the coming wave of Winterborn.

The sound of booted footsteps outside the chamber took Jax by surprise. He turned to the door as it swung open, and Brother Jon stepped through, newly arrived from the north.

"Where is everyone?" Jon snapped, not even offering Jax a greeting.

"Sarra has been challenged," replied the clerk, with a calmness he didn't feel.

"So?" Having been absent, Jon had no inkling of the process written in the Annals.

"So the Portioning is on hold until the Challenge has been tested. Prepare yourself for a new Knut."

"You believe the Challenge will succeed, then." It was not a question.

"They always have before. Obviously." Jax did not need to explain. If a Knut could prove victory over the waves, then his or her work would be done, atonement fulfilled.

"I suppose I shall have to give my report on the Fowker raid to the new Knut, then," said Jon, holding up the sheaf of papers in his hand. "Who made the challenge, by the way?"

"Goodwife Meryn," Jax replied. "An unlikely challenger, I know, but I sense she sees the currents beneath the surface, nonetheless. With her family all lost in San Peterpoll, I'm sure she'll be grateful for any light you can shed on the tragic events there." As he spoke, Jax noted a shadow of trepidation pass over Jon's face before he could compose himself. The clerk held out his hand, indicating Jon's documents. "I will need to make a copy for the Annals. I may as well start now whilst we're waiting."

Jon hesitated, but had no grounds to refuse the clerk's request. He handed over one sheet, and made to return the rest to his satchel, but Jax had already caught a glimpse of the document. "A list of names, Jon? You have already had time to consider names for the reassignment of holdings? Quick work, Jon. Very quick."

The sea's rise was inexorable, yet the waves were gentle as they began to caress her naked feet. The water was cold, but the beating sun warmed the air in the sheltered cove. A mercy or a torture, Sarra could not decide, because the warmth served to mark more sharply the waters' rise up her dangling legs, its pooling in the cold seat of the throne, the heavy clinging of the robes that it soaked.

Her voice was hoarse with pleading. All alone with her fate, no one else would ever know what she promised the Gods in return for forgiveness. History was replayed; the waters rose as they had risen over the lost lands, her pleas for life were the pleas of all of Linsey. Her flesh was the island itself, drowning slowly, inch by inch, condemned by the long forgotten, no longer understood transgressions of their forebears. All the sham of selfless ritual she had performed for countless thousands of tides was stripped back now to the fundamental question of survival.

Small things floated in the water's swell, brushing her skin, sneaking under the billowing robe where the caress of limp wrack stirred regrets and pride for her life of childless, necessary sacrifice. The rippling waters stirred her unsuckled breasts, laid a shimmering noose to her neck, and splashed on to her upturned, imploring face, then kissed her thin lips. She spluttered on the bitter brine and the sea entered her, but briefly. Satisfied, appeased, forgiving, the water began its slow, so slow, retreat.

Sarra breathed again, exulting in the receding caress of the defeated sea.

The sudden squall blew up out of nowhere, almost as though the sea raged against some distant slight. The fury of the westerly storm scattered the convoy of merchantmen in the darkness. The oar-slaves on the floundering ships fought all night against the crashing swell as the coxes tried to steer their ships into the howling winds. Prows rose and tumbled over the oncoming waves, wild even in the lee of the

Knotty Shore. Terror whipped the rowers' backs more harshly than slavemasters ever could, yet still the ships slipped ever eastward across the Trent Strait, pushed inexorably towards an uncertain fate.

Karel and his crewmates strained against the tempest as it drove their de-masted hulk further off course. They lost sight of the other ships, though whether across or beneath the waves they could neither tell nor care. The struggle itself was care enough.

The night was long and unnavigable with the stars hidden behind a shroud of angry cloud, but finally a spectral greyness lightened the eastern horizon. Ex-hausted, his back aching as much from the battering spray and chilling wind as from his exertions, Karel shook the stinging salt-water from his eyes to gaze upon the first rays of the new day's dawning.

Against the rising sun, the familiar profile of the Serpent's Back was silhouet-ted along the horizon. Karel could only pray the storm would grant them a safe landfall, and not dash the ship and his hopes upon the spuming rocks.

'NAUT

BY CATHERINE McGUIRE

The heat of July seeped into the overnight cool of the house. Sun sent glowing shafts under the gently stirring linen drapes. The straw tick rustled as Lawry rolled over and groaned. His head felt stung by nettles and pounded by bricks. The celebration had gone on too long and too intensely—he should have left when Marie did. He'd overslept, and she'd let him. Hell to pay later.

Slowly, achingly, he dressed, then carried the chamber pot out with him into the hall. He could hear little Matt and Jori happily shrieking in the kitchen and quickly changed his mind about breakfast. He tiptoed through the front door, walked around and emptied the pot in the privy. He threw down some sawdust, then set the pot on a barrel to rinse later. The sun felt good on his shirt as he awkwardly started to hoe weeds. The half-acre kitchen garden had an abundance of lettuce, peas, kale and cabbage; it was the season of fullness. In a minute, she'd glance out and bring him coffee—she was a wonderful wife, and he was grateful. Images swam up of last night's fete for Jon, the first returning USAnaut in ten years. Jon Jimson, his classmate through eight grades, always the crazy daring one—now suddenly back and the center of attention.

"Coffee?"

Marie had come up behind him, patted him on the shoulder. He gratefully accepted it, looked away from her thin-lipped expression. He probably had made some kind of fool of himself; not the first time. The last part of the party was pretty much a blank, but by the end of the day Lawry was sure he'd have heard it all. Very little slipped through the gossip mill's cracks. The bitter dandelion and chicory brew was almost too much for his shaky gut—Johnson's home brew had gone down so smooth, but stayed, like a vicious squatter, far too long.

"Marie, I'm sorry, I—"

She shrugged. Her straw-blonde hair was cut just under her ears for summer, freckles beginning to merge into a tan. She was still lithe and attractive after five years of marriage. He'd seen the eager eyes turned toward her last night. If he wasn't careful, she could be swept out of his life. He stretched his face into a smile, ignoring his throbbing head.

She said, "I'm taking Matt and Jori to Risa's, then I'll order flour down at the mill—can you get it before midmeal?"

"Yeah, no problem. I'll take a cartload of the birch to pay down some of it. Do you know if they want more potatoes?" Last harvest had been good, and there was still more than enough in the cellar.

"Well, I saw it on the list last Friday, so probably." He almost missed her brief smile as she quickly hugged him, then returned to the house. The sun started to bake off some of his hangover, seeping into his skin, beneficent and soothing. The odor of moist loam rose up like sweet perfume. Alone with his thoughts, Lawry hoed with more vehemence, as if the aching muscles could push away everything else. But his thoughts were relentless.

He had never wanted to be a 'Naut, but Jon had been brimming with plans since they were seven—how he'd go off on the long, lonely trek through wilderness, charting what was there and what wasn't anymore; mapping the places that might yield salvage, and the places too dangerous to go near; living on his wits and the small pack of precious tools to give him an edge against the barbarians. *Why aren't we called barbarians?* Lawry mused. Somehow, it was always the others. Lawry had studied to be a restorer, had apprenticed at 14, perfectly content to live within the known world. His parents were still alive; five sisters and brothers had 22 children, and the family gatherings were joyous. Martinsville had what he needed—the other villages came over to employ its ironworker, weavers, and medic. The mercantile was the largest in the district. Why give that up to risk death?

He hadn't even thought about any of this in three years; Jon's return had shaken something loose inside. Lawry drew his hoe carefully alongside young cabbage. Stories from last night coalesced from the inner fog. There was a big new city two weeks southeast of here, tucked up in the Cascade range, living off trade from various salvage claims, the 2,000 inhabitants surviving on greenhouse plants and goat meat. The elders would be sending an ambassador out soon.

Jon had sworn that there was a secret rendering plant in the city that simply recycled the inhabitants themselves—but of course they wouldn't admit to that, and he'd only heard it from an old hermit who lived a distance from the city called Crater.

"There certainly wasn't a big cemetery," he'd commented, as he'd told the tale to a mix of laughter and chilled silence. Lawry, who had been listening from a far corner, nursing his whiskey, remembered Jon's wild stories from school.

Another item that silenced the room was the *buffalope* spotting—Jon had brought home drawings of what he swore was an odd, long-legged, shaggy beast wandering east of the Great Desert, among the foothills of the Rockies. Nothing in the zoology lists matched it, and Jon's opinion was that it was a mutation wandered up from the nuked flats of California. Lawry wondered at that, too—although again, it sounded so much like Jon in the classroom.

But as the evening got fuzzier, Lawry found himself paying more attention to the joyous adulation; the excitement as if each person there had taken the trip. What did they get from it? He had hung out in the shadows, watching Marie chatting among the cooks, watching his neighbors slapping each other on the back and cheering each of the stories. What use were stories? The town survived because of farmers and the craftsfolk like the miller Shon, and Al the blacksmith, and Mina the glassblower. This wild adventure was so frivolous—but look at the welcome Jon got. A month's worth of food in one evening! *And* he would get a house, a garden plot and free medical for life. Lawry was sure Jon would have gone for nothing.

"So, how go the crops?" Jon's voice cut into his daydreaming; Lawry dropped the hoe and turned, stumbling slightly.

"Jon? Didn't you have a Q&A town hall today?" Lawry said. His voice rasped from a dry throat.

"I excused myself for a walk. Hadn't sat that long in years."

Jon had aged, that was clear—but still the same grin, the gray eyes part-closed in amusement. His blonde hair was halfway down his back in a braid; there was a scar on his right cheek and some of his right earlobe gone—that was the brigands he'd told about last night. He was as scrawny as ever, but more muscled. And some other indescribable difference. Lawry realized he was staring stupidly, and bent to pick up the hoe.

"It's—good to see you, Jon." *Was it?* He wasn't sure. "Glad you got home safe." That part was true.

Jon grinned wider. "Definitely times I wasn't sure I would . . . but what a country!" He took a breath, as if to begin recounting.

"What do you plan to do now?" Lawry cut in. He didn't need to hear more tales. Tales didn't grow cabbage. He slowly hoed out a few weeds while half-watching his friend.

"First, get re-acquainted with all my old friends." Jon waved his hand blithely, but there was a catch in his voice.

"Was it lonely out there?" That was what Lawry wanted most to know—how did Jon manage three years alone? Three years without women. Probably.

Jon looked around, found a wooden box, carried it over and sat down beside the end row. That nudged Lawry—"I'm sorry. Would you like coffee or tea? We have mint, chamomile . . ." he trailed off, mind blanking. His head still hurt, and he vaguely blamed his friend.

"Nothing, thanks. I was hoping to say hello to Marie—is she here?"

The fear he had stomped on last night came up like old whiskey. "Uh, no—she's dropping the two boys off at sprout school and putting in the milling order. Knowing Marie, she'll be gone for a couple hours, visiting her sister. Didn't—didn't you see her last night?" Marie certainly remembered greeting Jon; she repeated the story twice after Lawry got home.

Jon shrugged. "I guess. There was so much going on. A bit overwhelming, to be honest—after all that time alone." That was it—there was a streak of sadness that he'd never noticed in Jon before. "There weren't as many towns as the map said there'd be . . . well, *they* were still there—but the people were gone." He frowned, kicked the dirt with his heel. "Lots of animals, birds—but if I ran into twenty occupied towns in a year, that was a lot."

"I'm not sure I wanted to know that."

"I'm not sure *I* wanted to know that." Jon laughed, without humor. "I had a different sense of the world before I left." He shook himself. "But tell me what you've been up to for eight years? We haven't talked since I went into 'naut school."

Lawry winced. "What can I say? Hoeing cabbage, making or fixing furniture for those who can afford it. Three children; two alive." He shrugged—embarrassed, annoyed. "Life doesn't change much here."

"Right—old Morgan took you on as apprentice before I went into training—I remember now! Is he still as crazy as he always seemed when he taught shop?"

"Old Morgan died last winter. Flu. I guess I'm master now . . . not that I have his skills."

Jon was silent, his face looked almost panicky. "Well, sure—they would have to . . ." he muttered, looking away. Louder, he asked, "What about Old Man Dyskstra? And Harpy Williams? I—I didn't see them at the party last night."

"Dyskstra hasn't left his bed for about eight months. Widow Williams died two years ago. That's her cabin you're getting." They stared at each other.

"Oh. I guess I have some catching up to do."

"Odd that they don't make that part of the debrief."

Jon frowned. "These two weeks of quarantine, they mostly wanted to listen to me. Guess they figured the townsfolk would fill me in. Or maybe they didn't want to hit me with too much." He jumped up. "Guess I'd better get back. They're gonna think I ran away." Jon grinned, walked over and gave him a fast hug, to Lawry's shock, then hurried away with a wave, calling back, "Say hey to Marie for me!"

After Jon had vanished around the hedge, Lawry put down the hoe and went inside. He needed more coffee.

‡‡‡

There was plenty of time to examine the alternating fallow and cropped fields as Marie walked the boys to the weekly part-lessons, part-playtime that everyone called "sprout school." Matt was four and Jori three—they walked slow. She checked her stride, feeling antsy, trying to be patient. Jori of course had to have one of every weed and plant he saw. Possibly he would follow her as herbalist. He already knew which plants not to touch or eat. Matt preferred to search for birds and animals, looking for spoor and glimpses of wild creatures. It was a fairly solitary walk along a private dirt path that cut across the fields, and sliced a quarter mile off the trip. When the path finally ended on the broad Tan Creek Road, Marie made the boys walk close to her. Too often horsemen careened along here like deer fleeing a cougar.

A half-mile later, the smithy's dark smoke was visible, and the shacks of Martinsville's humble folk crowded the road, the easier for their occupants to pop out and beg a little of travellers. Marie hated this part of the walk, even though none of the humble folk had dared ask her for anything in the past few years. They knew better. Still, she picked Jori up and hurried Matt a little as they passed one room stick-and-daub boxes, poorly thatched and leaning, their narrow windows and doors merely curtained. Beyond them, the town proper started: mud-plaster and straw cob on the bones of the former city; a few stone buildings, mostly one story or wood for the second floor. The place looked like a coat that had gone at the cuffs and collar, and was patched on top of its patches. Dust from the road tinged everything, the townsfolk reasoned, so why go to the huge expense of painting? Some of the homes had colored curtains, a rare few had glass in the windows and the cobbler had a tiny blue shoe dangling over the door. That was all. It grated on her. Sometimes when she walked, she imagined the town colored like the meadow flowers—pink, yellow, azure, purple. Streets of color and life! Instead, she had this dingy huddle of houses, supposedly the biggest town in the district? Five streets one way, three the other . . . ringed with ruins, gardens, farms and the more pungent businesses such as the tanner's.

Shaking herself out of it, Marie turned left on Second. As Matt recognized Risa's, he started running. She let a wriggling Jori down to run after his brother and watched as they were let in to the low-fenced yard by Risa's tween daughter Pat. Marie waved at Pat and the boys, and retraced her steps. The mill was at the base of Fourth, by the river it needed to operate. But even the short half-mile to the mill would take an hour, since her sister Janni lived on Fourth and brother Tad worked at the salvage shop on Pitt. There would be no excuse good enough if they found out she'd passed them by!

Janni's two-story house was wedged between the weaver's and the medic's. A pre-Chaos "relic," it had brick walls, fine wood trim, but of course only oiled paper in the windows. The door was open, with just a thin linen screen, to give more light and air.

"Hi, sis!" Marie called out as she hurried past the elegant staircase, down the hall to the kitchen where Janni's voice echoed reply.

"Hi, Marie! Have you come to give me a hand with the washing?"

Their old joke; as children, they'd fought bitterly about who had to pound the clothes on the river rocks. Marie usually lost even though she was the elder.

Janni was mixing up a batch of bread on the kitchen counter, up to her elbows in flour, while five-year old Gert sat at the table, braiding strips of scrap linen. Her tiny fingers swiftly flipped the free ends of cloth, over-under-over, until the strips were nearing the end. Then she groped along the table for more strips. Blind from birth, Gert was learning the rug trade.

"Why weren't you at the fest last night?" she asked Janni. "The stories were just amazing!"

"Oh . . . ah. Well, I guess it was hard to think about listening to Jon, with Mick still . . ."

Marie bit her lip. "Yes. Sorry." She should have remembered about Janni's brother-in-law. Jon was the first of the five 'nauts to return; now the "countdown" would become more acute for those waiting for the others. She tried to speak lightly. "Well, Jon's known for his wild stories, and last night he had some real 'rageous ones! Like a mutant buffalo rabbit, and people living in a raft city on a huge lake."

Janni piled the dough into a bowl, covered it with a damp cloth and set it aside to rise. "I'm *so* not surprised. Walk with me to the pump? Gert, honey, we'll be right back."

Marie followed her out back, along the alley. Sunny, wide enough for bulky re-cycling carts, the alley was treacherous with broken asphalt and smelled faintly of sewage. The compost buckets by each door were the obvious reason. Only one of the back doors was open; old Syl was shelling beans in her doorway. She looked up as they passed but didn't wave. *Sour old woman*, Marie thought.

"Yes, Jon seemed an odd choice to me. How will we ever know what's real?" Janni continued.

"I heard they have a drug that will make him tell the truth," Marie commented. "They only use it on 'nauts."

"Oh, come on! That's an old guys' tale."

Elder Marc was filling his two wooden buckets; Janni waited until he was done and around the corner before she continued.

"Are you still fond of him?" she asked. "Are you sorry—"

Marie shook her head to forestall the question. "No. Jon was funny and some-times he could be really generous—but he was always too wild. That is not a 'set-tling man.' I wonder if he'll even be able to stay long."

"Even with the free house and garden? He'd have his pick of the single women."

"Oh, he might get married. But that wouldn't keep him, I'm guessing."

Janni looked shocked. They had reached her door; she glanced back inside, then lowered her voice. "He wouldn't just leave, would he?"

"I don't think he knows his mind. He might have the best intentions, but . . ." Marie shrugged.

Lawry was washing up the breakfast dishes when Gordon Allen poked his head in at the kitchen door. Catching sight of Lawry at the sink, the old man hobbled in, already starting to describe his order. *Not a man of small talk*, Lawry thought.

" . . . and if you can use the old back and insides, that would be good."

"Hi, Gordie—take a seat. Would you like tea? Is this about the dresser you wanted me to repair?"

"No, it's not, son—weren't you listening?" The old man rested his thin backside on the bench. "I bought an old rocker washer from that salvager who came through last month. It's got a perfect cradle and the gears seem to be free of cracks—but the outside got broke somehow. You're the only furnituresmith worth taking it to. The curved sides might be hard to rebuild, but you might be able to reuse part of them. I'm hoping to gift it to Sukey for her birthday."

Ah, his daughter. She took in washing, and a rocker-washer would make much easier work.

"Well, I'll have to look at it before I can give you a trade-price. Can I come by this afternoon? I have to go to town before mid-meal, but I'm free after that."

"That would be fine, son." Gordon was already up and away, hobbling out the door. He was the perfect cemetery custodian, despite his limp. He lived happily alone on the far side of Cooper Hill, unworried by the thought of bandits, bears or bogeymen.

A rocker-washer would be a challenge. Lawry smiled as he considered it. He'd seen a couple of those sketched out in old books, and once in a news sheet brought by a traveller. He heard they were restored to use when the worst of the Chaos had settled and people started to think about how to live better. The pictures he'd seen had been too hard to copy. Maybe he'd have better luck with this one and could make a few more.

Tossing the breakfast scraps to the chickens, he noticed the sundial showed 10:30. Sleeping in had knocked off his sense of time. He hurried to the shed, hitched Beast to the cart and led him across the large yard to the woodpiles. It was hot work stacking the flatbed, and he made sure to fill his canteen from the pump before heading into town. Drinking deeply, he had a sudden resurgence of tipsy light-headedness. Damn his idiotic drinking! He laid the sack of potatoes on the seat, with the top tied to the footrail. The large truck tires, patched with spare rubber, wobbled more than usual. The left front needed inflating; he'd have to stop at the smith's and use their air pump. The fact that Oak Crest Road was still a washboard from the rough winter didn't help matters. Lawry was forced to slow Beast to a walk to avoid breaking an axle or strut. Fran's hayfields passed slowly by, followed by Lou's corn. He could see Lou and his son at the far side of the field and he waved. This was the kind of morning that he lived for, if only the little nagging worry—and his headache—would subside.

The impromptu houses of the humble folk came into view. Lawry recognized the walnut stained planks he'd helped pull out of the old library after it burned. Joseph Crane's old mantelpiece was now a door lintel, which always amused Lawry to see. He tossed three potatoes to Lin, Brody and Shirl, and they waved and sang their thanks.

"Save it for the travellers," he laughed. He didn't need a performance. He steered Beast carefully down the main street, shooing the dogs, pigs and stray children aside with gentle nudges of his whip. The sunlight gleamed on the soft weathered wood buildings, and the scent of baking mixed with the coal smoke of Al's smithy.

At the mill, he was happy to trade out the wood and potatoes for the full order. Marie had gotten ten pounds of oats and twenty of wheat. Shon was too rushed to regale Lawry with tales of last night's drunken spree, for which Lawry was grateful. He hoisted the sacks into the cart bed, put a feedbag on Beast, and sat for a moment, watching the mill wheel and listening to the river. The Willette ran straight and deep here; a little more narrow than at Honeyvale where Marta's ferry took traders across and down to Springfield. Up here, there was nothing to see on the other side but a lanky maple and alder forest springing up where the Burn had taken most of the cedars. He could hear the town behind him, muffled shouts and laughter, and old man Jesey cursing out his mule again. Lawry grinned, then frowned. *If only Jon hadn't* . . . but it was evil to think that. It sure complicated things, though.

He heard the buzz of a crowd, and realized the Q&A had let out for mid-meal. He'd better move fast, to get this flour home in time! Then he caught sight of Marie walking along Main with Janni and Gert, a gaggle of children like sheep herded before them. He hailed them and stopped to lift his boys into the bed, nestled among the sacks, and to help Marie up onto the seat. Now the ride could be as leisurely as needed. He hugged her one-armed, and was thrilled by her warm smile. Maybe all was forgiven.

Just outside of town, he heard running boots behind, and the boys cried out, "Jay! Jay!" In a moment, the cart shook as Jared scrambled aboard. Lawry turned and grinned at his nephew. "What's your hurry?"

"Could you drop me at Lou's? I'm supposed to be helping with the weeding." Jared, 14, was almost as tall as Lawry. There was more scuffling as Jared rough-housed with the boys, who giggled and yelled. "Did you get to hear Jon today? I sat through all morning! That's why I'm late," he said. "Jon said there's a new town down in the Gold Hills—"

"Yes, he mentioned that last night." Lawry was startled at his own harsh voice. He softened. "Did he mention the buffalope?"

"Oh, yeah—he had to tell that one twice! And a mountain of glass bottles just over the mountains that are just over the hills . . . that's far away, isn't it?"

"Yup. That's far away. Probably too far for salvage."

"Miguel doesn't think so. He was talking about getting a wagon train star-ted—Jon thinks they could re-blaze an old logging trail and bring carts through. Think about all those bottles! Even the broke ones Miz Mina could melt down for slag! Miguel says he wants real windows in his house," Jared finished with a laugh.

Lawry dropped his nephew at Lou's, and told the boy to come by for supper. After unloading the food, then riding over to Gordon's to pick up the rocker-washer, he spent the day repairing an ornate glass-front dresser that was missing the glass, but would look otherwise as good as new, once he mixed the right stain to turn the pine to rosewood.

That evening at supper, Jared was still full of Jon's 'nautical adventures. Lou had been one of the debriefers, and let drop a few juicy morsels, apparently. The house was oppressive with the heat of cooking, so they had moved the table into the back yard. Jared flicked flies off his meal as he enthused.

"Lou said Jon admitted he once went totally crazy and started hacking down an empty house! And dressing up in other people's clothes!" Jared was a bit hard to un-derstand with his mouth full of turnip.

"Well, if they didn't have a serum in him, I wouldn't take a bet on that," Mar-ie commented with a laugh.

No breeze stirred, but the cedar's shade was cool. Matt and Jori wriggled on either side of Jared—as bouncy as baby chicks, Lawry thought fondly. Marie passed the big oak bowl of potatoes, and the smaller blue ceramic bowl of shredded goat cheese. Lawry took big helpings of each—he felt hollowed out after not being able to eat most of the day.

"What's a se-er rum?"

"Nothing," Lawry answered quickly, glancing at his wife. *Do you want to get into that?*

Marie distracted the boy with a chicken leg; the old Orp hen was not tender, but better than squirrel.

Jared veered onto another thought. "Paul said they'd be starting another 'naut school in five years. They'll be sending out more 'nauts when I'm 23—I'd be old enough! Paul's gonna sign up, too."

"Jared!" Lawry set down his fork with a thump. "I thought you were apprenticing to the miller!"

"Yeah, well?"

"Well, you can't just go off after you've learned a trade! Miller Shon will be depending on you then."

Jared persisted, "Why can't I become a 'naut?"

Lawry could see himself ten years from now, waving goodbye to his favorite nephew. *No!*

"Training is tough, Jay. It's five years of little trips, going out a little farther each time, learning how to survive. And only five get picked to go, after all that work. In Jon's class, they only trained twenty; nine dropped out or were expelled, and two . . . were killed."

"Killed in school? How?"

Lawry cleared his throat, glancing at the two boys who were luckily distracted by suet pudding. Marie's face was unreadable. "They don't say. 'Naut school is pretty private. They don't like the idea of just anyone going out on a Search. So what happens in the school stays there."

"They have magic tools, huh?"

"Not magic." Lawry stifled a chuckle. "Things like a geiger counter, a rifle with a little telescope, glasses that let you see in the dark, and lamps that run on the sun—they're from the old time. We keep losing a few each Search, so that's another reason they have to be careful who they send."

"Was Jon the only one they sent?"

"No, don't you remember the ceremony? You were 11 at the time. Five went out—so far, he is the only return. But it's early; only three years. It's possible that Garry, Jud, Mick and Lori will still come back."

"They'll get a hero's welcome, too, huh?"

"Yeah."

An unreasonable anger was building inside. Why did they enchant young kids with this wanderlust, and send them out into god-knows-what every ten years? What was so damned important out there? Lawry cleared the table and washed the dishes, refusing all offers of assistance. He felt too sour to be around others.

There was an almost palpable anticipation in the town, as everyone looked for the next 'naut to arrive. A week passed with nothing more exciting than Jon escorting Shawna, the mayor's daughter, to the Friday dance. Then Lori appeared at the medic's, very gaunt and with her left arm hanging useless. She was immediately placed in quarantine, but her parents and brother spoke with her daily through the glass-paned isolation room as the town again buzzed with the second 'naut's return.

Lawry couldn't hide a sense of desolation. How long before the town returned to normal? What if it never did? He tried to remember thirteen years back—he had been 11—when the last 'nauts had returned. But only two had—that was what he remembered most. Three simply had not come back, and three families, and many friends, had gone into a slow, extended mourning as the chances of return got slimmer and slimmer. The whole town grieved for at least a year, and the two other 'nauts—Jim and Inger—retreated into a kind of guilty isolation, as if it had been their fault. Jim later moved to Grantsville, 35 miles away, and Inger never married, becoming a kind of hermit. Lawry couldn't remember the last time he'd seen her in town. She certainly hadn't been at Jon's party.

That evening, after the worst of the heat had eased, Lawry cut and brought a downed maple from the woods to the yard and began to split the rounds. Marie had put the boys to bed, and was raking out the chicken coop, carrying the soiled straw in the wheelbarrow over to the compost. Lawry glanced over and was startled to see her catch the rake on the coop door, then raise it as if she were going to throw it, before she stopped herself and bent over the barrow.

"Are you alright, Marie?"

She jerked upright, then turned with a smile. "Yes, just a long day, I guess."

Always a long day recently, he thought. *For both of us.*

"Anything particular?"

She sighed and he braced himself. *She doesn't want to hurt me. This is going to be about Jon.*

"You know that Harvest caravan to Springfield?"

"The one the craft and farmers' trade group plans every October?"

"Yeah. Well . . ." she turned to face him. "Have you ever thought about going with them?"

He blinked. "Me?"

"Not just you—all of us."

"What—Matt and Jori, too? Why?"

"I dunno—just to see it."

"See *what*?" He'd lost the thread; where did Jon come in?

"Just the big city and another part of this country, and maybe another small town in between . . ." she trailed off, seeing his puzzlement and biting her lip. "Never mind. Doesn't matter."

He walked over to the coop. Her face was smudged; he pulled his handkerchief out and gently rubbed the dirt off.

"It *does* matter. But I don't understand. Why do you want to see another town? This one is just fine."

"It is not! It looks like a dog with mange! We don't even have a proper main street—just a row of slightly bigger *shacks*!" Marie's voice ended in a shriek, and even she looked shocked. Lawry was stunned.

"What—what's wrong with Main Street?" *Where did that tirade come from?? Jon!* It must have been Jon's stories that had soured her. He'd never heard Marie complain before, about the town at least.

Marie turned back to the coop. "It's small and dinky and . . . and just for once, I want to see a proper town!" Her shoulders curved forward, and he recognized her defeated stance. She would get like this at her folks' place, after some battle over kids or cooking or . . . just anything. He hesitated, then placed his hand lightly on her shoulder. What could he say?

"Marie, I *know* you wouldn't want me to leave the crops. Do you want to go . . . alone? To Springfield?"

He fought to keep his hand from clenching. He wanted to break Jon into little bits right now. Springfield was just Martinsville bigger—and probably dirtier and more worn out, with fifteen hundred residents! He'd heard Kerm talk about it last year after the trading delegation got back. It didn't sound like much. But there was no telling Marie when she got hard and set like this. But what if she went and didn't come back?

She stepped away from his hand, turned and attempted a smile. "No, of course not. I couldn't leave the boys, or the canning. If this is another odd summer like last year, even setting the trip into October won't be far enough past harvest. Only singles are going on this trip—and the widowed." A spasm of pain crossed her face. "I should have gone before we got married, so I could've said I'd done it." Both of them remembered why that wouldn't have worked—Lila, now five years buried up at Cooper Hill. Life shat on them in so many ways.

Jori's thin wail coming from the house ended the discussion; Marie hurried in the back door. Lawry stood a moment, feeling like a tree eaten hollow from the inside. Damn Jon Jimpson to the bottom of Hell! A small voice suggested it could have been worse if Jon hadn't gone to 'naut school, but Lawry pushed it down vehemently and stormed into his workshop.

Inside, Marie bent over Jori as he finally closed his eyes. She stroked his fine hair. Where would *he* go when he grew up? Was he stuck in this town too, or was there a chance for him to find something better? In a world as vast as the one they were supposedly living in, could she help him avoid being just a weed puller or iron pounder? She remembered Lawry's face just now—his deep puzzlement. *There* was a man who was content with his lot in life! Why couldn't she be that way? She had been so jealous when Jon and the others left on their adventure—even before that. When they were taking volunteers, at 15, she had come *so* close to putting her name in! She glanced down at the boys, curled like puppies on their twin bunks, wrapped in wool blankets Marie's mother had woven. She loved them more than Life itself, and wished she could put to rest the part of her that needed to know what the world looked like. But it was still there, as strong as it had been when she was a girl, when five-year-old Marie had almost made it to the next town before frantic neighbors had hunted her down. *Why* hadn't she tried again? Then she remembered the cruel whispering about those who had volunteered for 'Naut school. Praised as heroes, and gossiped about as misfit, mentally odd. And as a tween, it had been so important that others liked her. "What a mess of pottage I settled for," she murmured.

Lawry hid out in his workshop all the next day, telling himself it would do no good to reason with Marie in that mood. He planed a curly maple board, admiring the intricate swirls. Why couldn't she be pleased with the beauty that surrounded them? She was a good woman and he had never regretted their lovemaking and subsequent marriage, but perhaps he should have gotten to know her better. These moods of hers hit him in the gut like a mule kick.

The rich aroma of cedar and pine mixed with the vinegary tang of wood stains. Dust motes shimmered in sun shafts; the plane whispered. This tiny workshop was almost filled with his worktable, the shelf of tools and the two pieces he was working on. He needed to double the space or move down to Morgan's old town shop, and he needed to do one of them soon. Being within earshot of Marie and the boys for five years had been worth the cramp, but was he squeezing out opportunities? And would there be fewer fights if he worked in town? But hadn't the fights mostly started after Jon got back? Jon was the spider cleverly weaving his spell on her . . . the plane jinked and gouged a strip from the maple. Lawry cursed. Jon was spoiling his work, too!

The next two weeks continued the hot, sunny weather, and began to put a strain on irrigation. Every last bit of wash water went onto the crops. Farmers began mixing urine straight into buckets of water, to increase the volume, and mule trains were sent up over Cooper Hill to capture kegs of Hadley River water. It was normal, but still tricky. Lawry kept a worried eye on the garden as he finished up several woodworking projects. The town seemed to be settling back into the routine, albeit with one ear cocked for any sign of the other 'nauts. Lori was due to come out of quarantine and be feted in four days. The delegation to Springfield had been picked and were discussing their preparations, with no further comment from Marie. But Lawry knew better than to think she had forgotten. The knot in his chest was growing as big as the heads of cabbage.

The rocker-washer was just about finished—it was a beautiful contraption, gleaming resin-soaked wood and shining brass bolts. The brass would tarnish, but right now it was a work of art, in Lawry's mind. He could ride it up to old Gordon in two days, once the resin coat was fully cured. Maybe he could ask Marie if she wanted one for herself . . . he had no clue what she really wanted. Would he ever?

Storm clouds began building on Friday, and on Saturday Lawry decided to get the washer up to the cemetery before the weather broke. At first light, he loaded the washer on the cart and tied it securely. It was slow moving up the lightly-travelled path so as not to wreck all his hard work, and he finally pulled into the cemetery close to noon. The sky was black along the southern horizon and the wooden grave markers, and beyond them Gordon's house of gray fieldstone glowed white as sun glared down on the field, as if furious at being pushed aside. The humidity was intense; Lawry and Beast both dripped sweat.

Gordon helped Lawry unload the washer from the cart and into the shed by the house.

"You did a *fine* bit of work here, youngster!" Gordon exclaimed as they got it safely under the roof. "Sukey is gonna be just beside herself!" Obviously he was giving himself equal credit, but Lawry didn't mind. "Come inside for a drink before you go back."

Lawry accepted gratefully; he led Beast over to the trough before following Gordon into the house. Inside was blessedly cool and dark; the front room, as kitchen and living area, had three windows but only one of the heavy shutters was opened and sunlight shimmered on the varnished table near it. Gordon brought a pitcher and two cups over to the table. The ale must have been fresh from the root cellar, as it was cold and delicious.

Gordon waited until Lawry took his first few gulps to lean forward, his expression grim. "I'm not one to spook at shadows," he said, "but I'm almost sure there's a band of thieves over the hill."

"*What?*" Lawry put down his cup. "Have you seen them?"

Gordon shrugged. "Nope. Just smelled smoke and heard the echoes of them rustling around in the hollow just past Boyd's Peak."

Squinting out the window, Lawry could just about see the little rocky outcrop named for Boyd Hardy, who'd been thrown by a horse from it and died about 40 years ago. Lawry had only been up that road once at fifteen, on a long trip to plead for planting seeds from Spruceton, after most of Martinsville's spring crop had been washed out. He barely remembered the scrub-tangled dip in the ground just past the peak, but he recalled his uncle's warning about being alert for thieves at that spot. He remembered being hungry that year, too. Spruceton had been grudging, but it was enough. Barely.

He didn't want to distrust the man, but Gordon's house—the cemetery guard house—had been built generations ago as an outpost of the town, and thick as it was, would any such far-away sounds reach? And could it have been noises from Martinsville? Echoes were tricky that way. But he didn't say that.

"Do you want me to tell the sheriff for you? I'll be in town today."

The old man moved his cup around the table. "Aw, I don't know that I want to call out the volunteers 'til I know a bit more. Maybe just one or two scouts."

"We don't do it like that, you know, Gordie. Safety in numbers." But the image of Jon creeping through the underbrush came unbidden to him. His renegade heart leapt. Jon would love to scout this! Town gossip was that Jon was bored and cranky in his free homestead, chafing at the town niceties. And if Jon was ambushed . . . ?

"Well! I'll be going back, then." Lawry jumped up, startled at how loud the statement came out. What the hell was happening to him? He gulped the last bit of ale and shook Gordon's hand. "I hope Sukey is really happy with your gift."

The drive home was a pitched inner battle, like a ferocious town council of partisan thoughts. Jon would jump at this chance! Jon had no right, nor Lawry, to go rogue like that. Dangling vine maples slashed at his head; sun flickered and jumped in thickets. Time to re-cut this trail. Jon would thank him for telling him about this. Jon was the only person in town with enough training to handle a scout trip. Lawry was a nasty sonofabitch for even toying with the idea. How could all these statements be true? By the time Lawry got back to his land, he had a throbbing headache.

He felt chilled when he discovered Marie had invited Jon to dinner that night. It was almost like a set-up, but he didn't know by whose hand. He watched dully as she put a slab of salt pork on to boil with cabbage and potatoes; it probably was the last hock of the winter. His resentment bubbled like the water on the stove. Luckily the boys were loudly racing around the table; their exuberance was a welcome distraction.

Jon arrived a half-hour early, just as the storm's rumbles turned to pattering rain. Lawry tapped a small keg of Marsha's golden ale and the three adults sat on the kitchen porch, within earshot of the boiling dinner, watching the boys race around in the cooling downpour.

"Rain came not a minute too soon," Jon said, leaning his chair back and lifting his ale in toast.

"It's needed, certainly. I suppose this is too quiet for you, after—after your adventure?" Marie asked.

Jon looked down, considering, then shook his head. "No—it's a nice rest after a long trek. One can't spend all the time running away from bandits." They laughed; Lawry's was forced.

"Funny you mention that—" the words burst out. "Old Gordie thought he heard some bandits up past Boyd's Peak the last few days." His chest tightened. He'd done it now.

Jon looked as eager as a hound dog, "Really? Just up over the ridge? What did the sheriff say?"

"Lawry—you didn't mention that!" Marie cried. "That's too close for comfort! You should have said!"

"Gordie's not sure he's right; it's just some noise and maybe a woodfire's smoke. He didn't want to get out the volunteers until he was more sure. It's nothing to worry about, I'm sure." Damned if he did and damned if he didn't.

Marie shook her head. "Well, I'm keeping the boys a lot closer to me, and I don't want you going too far off, until somebody finds out for sure. There's only the Davidsons between us and the cemetery."

Lawry risked a side glance at Jon; he was sipping his ale, looking off into the woods. Finally, Jon commented, "It wouldn't take much. Just wander up there quietly; wouldn't even have to get too close. I got pretty good at sensing anything I wanted to avoid."

There—he'd taken the hint. Lawry felt as miserable as when he baited the mole traps. But like Jon said, he'd gotten good at surviving, and who else would be able to scout out something that might be a danger to the town?

Lawry set aside his ale. It tasted sour. Dinner was subdued, and even the boys seemed to recognize something was wrong.

That evening, in bed, Lawry held Marie against his chest, feeling her breath. Was hers as constricted as his felt?

"Marie, I don't want him to go alone. I'll tell the sheriff tomorrow."

She sighed. "It won't make any difference. He's probably already on his way up there tonight."

"No! In the rain? You think? Would he just—" But of course he would. "He should know that's not how we do it. There's safety in numbers."

"But he just proved there's also safety in singles." She shifted and eased herself out of his embrace. "He's been as restless as a leashed dog, and now you've thrown him a big stick."

"Marie, I'm sorry—I didn't—"

"Didn't you? But it doesn't matter. Can't you feel it? Jon can't come home again. Maybe there *is* no home for him anymore. Maybe *that's* why we shouldn't go away." That last sentence was mumbled half to herself but Lawry caught it and froze.

"Sweetie, I know you were fond of him—or are—or . . ." he trailed off.

She turned back and nestled against his chest. "Jon hasn't changed since we were younger. I chose *you* back then . . . and that hasn't changed either."

Lawry couldn't find a reply. But his dreams that night were wild and dark.

The next day, as the storm passed to the north, leaving puddles and dripping trees, he did go into town, hunting down Sheriff Hal. But only after he'd broken a chair spindle, gouged two holes out of a nice pine board and slammed a hammer down on his finger. The day was ruined, and maybe he was cursed. Not that he was superstitious. But he needed to get free of this.

Hal was mending a book in the small room that housed rescued books from the old library fire. He agreed to send a group out to Boyd's Peak, and accepted Lawry's volunteering to be one of them. Every time Lawry tried to bring up Jon, it stuck in his throat. In the end, he figured he'd just wait and see.

It was late afternoon before they were riding up Cooper Hill, through dappled shade on the vined-over dirt road to the cemetery. With Lawry was Gerry, Hal, old Ron the tanner, and Margaret, Gene's daughter who, at twenty, had surpassed all the other militia candidates this year. All of them had long hardwood pikes, a few had knives in their belts, and Gerry had his short bow, in case they met resistance. They joked as they rode, but when they stopped to get an update from Gordon, they treated his descriptions with serious consideration. A five minute canter took them up to Boyd's Peak, where they slowed and moved as quietly as a group of five could. They paused where the road began to dip.

"There's an old fire smell, but nothing fresh—ya think?" Hal asked quietly.

Nods all around. Lawry picked up the tang of washed-down campfire; he relaxed. They rode another 25 yards into the valley, the horses picking their way carefully down the pebble-slick path. The smell grew stronger and Hal signaled the others to dismount. Lawry reluctantly held the horses as the others crept into the dripping underbrush. But in a few minutes, he heard them speaking in normal tones. A rustle and the scuffing of boots, and they came back through the underbrush. Maggie held a partly burnt bone that looked like deer.

"There was a crew, but they cleared off," Hal said, taking his reins again. "Maybe there about a week; didn't even leave much garbage. Definitely about five campers."

"Can I go look?" Lawry knew he sounded like a boy, but he had to know, and it was too late now to mention Jon. Giving Beast's reins to Maggie, Lawry ducked and scrambled into the campsite.

The fire pit was stone-ringed and full of wet ash. A deer had been sectioned and most of it cooked, the legs and head off to one side, partly gnawed by animals. Tamped-down brush in a ring around the firepit suggested at least five sleepers. Lawry inspected each area, looked as far as he could into the dense thickets, but there was nothing at all that showed Jon had been there. No broken brambles leading to a dead body, no fresh-dug grave or discarded shoe that he could recognize—nothing. He'd been crazy to think it. Guilt, relief and fear washed over him like bursts of storm. Jon had not been here, or if he had, he'd left with no trace. Probably he was back at his house and getting ready for dinner. Lawry rushed back up to the road, feeling a silly grin spread on his face.

"Okay—well, it was worth checking out, right?" he asked. They assured him it was.

"I'll be sending a group up around here more often," Hal said as they rode home.

Once Jon hadn't been seen for three days, the speculation that he had snugged up with a woman turned to more serious talk. Lawry, in the process of moving his workshop into town, had ample chance to hear the rumors and speculations. The leaden feeling returned; he reminded himself that there had been no sign of Jon at the campsite. Which meant very little. He teetered on panic the first two days, watching Marie for signs of worry. As the talk turned, she did get more serious, but didn't mention their conversation about the bandits.

Finally, the pressure inside was worse than over-fermented ale. He caught her alone in the afternoon and blurted, "Do you remember talking to Jon about the . . . about Gordie seeing . . ." It caught in his throat again.

"Yes, I remember," she said quietly. "I figured if you'd seen anything, you would have said."

Lawry nodded emphatically. "Yes. I looked hard at the site, and there was no sign at *all* that he'd been there." He started to sweat. Did he want to know what she thought?

She smiled, though her eyes were somber. "My guess is he used it as an excuse to get out of town."

"*What??*"

She chuckled wryly. "I *told* you he was like a leashed dog. Jon never was the settling type. I'm guessing he realized that he'd have to stay here out of gratitude for all the free stuff, and he was already beginning to feel smothered. Maybe he figured he'd look like a hero if he disappeared while going after bandits."

Lawry blinked. Jon—run off? Not dead in the bushes somewhere? Was that *possible?* The new scene imposed itself on his memory of events—a weird twin to his first scenario—all the same bits adding up to something wildly different. For a moment, he felt like he wanted to scream, like a boiler bursting. Then Marie wrapped her arms around him, and he felt her warm hair just under his chin. He hugged her fiercely and closed his eyes. *Saved.*

"Marie—if you really, *really* want to see Springfield, I'll bet we can find a time, before the spring planting next year—the winter root traders go down . . ."

She looked up at him with tears in her eyes. "Yes—I guess I would." She paused. "In a way, I wish I had volunteered to be a 'naut—"

"No!"

"Let me finish," she said. "I see now that it would have probably ruined me like Jon, if I'd even come back. But some of us can't help wondering what is over the hill or down the river."

"So it never was about Jon?"

She shook her head, stroked his cheek. "No, not him. What he *did*. What he got to see. But he paid a price. None of the 'nauts came back normal, did they?"

"No," he murmured into her soft hair.

"So that was too much—but just a little further, maybe that's all it will take. And then I'll see how much I have here."

"Or maybe this town will seem even smaller."

She shrugged helplessly. "I won't know until I see what happens. Maybe I just need that one little visit. Haven't you ever needed something so bad you were willing to risk everything?"

He caught his breath. The way she looked at him—did she know? She must! And was giving him a chance to make amends, to go with her on her journey, wherever it led.

He pulled her closer, so she couldn't see his expression. So many conflicting emotions! His comfortable life teetering, as he realized he had been treating Marie as just another part of his well-known and comfortable surrounds. He'd just assumed she was as satisfied; apparently not. Or not completely.

"Then we'll go, Marie. Anyway, my home is wherever you are."

"And you're my home, too." She looked up with a grin. "And we'll have some stories to tell at the solstice fest." She paused. "I'm not asking you to move, and I know this is risky. We can leave the boys with my sister, or yours. And I can bring an awful lot of herbs in one sack—we might actually make money." She smiled again, but her face held a question.

And once again Lawry didn't know the answer. Wasn't even sure he knew the question. Did they really want two different lives? Was there a way to weave the two together? The world was bigger than he wanted it to be, and that included the world inside.

"Lawry," she tapped him on the arm, "we will make this work. Maybe Jon brought us a gift, without realizing it. The best way to find weeds is when they're small. I shouldn't have kept my needs from you for so long. That was my fault. Thank you for hearing me now."

He squeezed her so tight she gasped. "And thank you . . . for—" He didn't have any good words. "Just for being you."

Jon had said he'd had a different sense of the world before going out. Wilderness had changed him. And Jon had brought back wilderness, strangeness . . . and the strangest bit of all had turned out to be inside Lawry. And once you'd experienced wilderness, there was no going back.

COYOTE YEAR
BY G. KAY BISHOP

When the earthquakes started up in February, I knew it was going to be a ba— I mean, an especially challenging year. Not that the quakes would do us much physical harm; even though our summer homes are raised on poplar and cypress poles, they are rooted more or less in thick mud. The mud would crack before the houses did. They would probably still be standing when we went to the bottoms for spring planting. I hoped. I hoped *and* prayed. Time spent rebuilding shelters would be time lost from field planting.

When I brought Winona her "hot mush" breakfast, she more or less confirmed my uneasy feelings. Poor kid seemed to catch every flu bug every winter, but so far she had always pulled through, since we first pulled her out of the belly of her poor mauled mother. Wild dogs. I shot twenty-five of them in a cold fury until one of my own clan came to calm me down. We had a heavy peppering of TriMeds among our relations. They saved the child but not the mother. I buried her in a magnificent robe of dogskins. The meat and bones went to feed the coyotes, who left our sheep alone that winter.

It was the same set of medical maven relations who had developed this tried and tested formula for winter catarrhs. It involved dried mushroom, goldenseal, echinacea and a smattering of various mints. I do not know what all was in it; but I know it was expensive to make and that I was considered a fool for buying it for a crippled child instead of saving it for myself. It took her fever down, though, and I was glad. I used the cheaper beer-mush antibiotic to clear up my less serious bronchial cough.

She looked better in body but troubled in soul. I got her to sit up, wrapped in a freshly laundered silk-lined blanket—I paid for that too; I am too old to be pounding wet blankets in winter—while I changed her dirty bed linen, put in place a clean chamberpot under the child-sized stool, and aired the snug room out a bit. When I was done, she had eaten every bite of the barley-corn-oat and last-of-the-honey pudding and licked the bowl clean too.

"Well, child," said I, "You may be blind, lame, halt, hare-lipped and half-albino, but you sure have a good appetite."

She giggled. She is quite used to me and my bad-taste jokes.

"Nana," she said seriously, detaining me with one claw hand as she gave me back the empty bowl, "it's a C-c-coyote year. He spat in the beer barrel and w-w-w-winked at me."

"Oho, so you caught that too, did you? Yes, I reckon we'll have to tread wary to keep out of Coyote's way this year. You be sure and tell me if he says anything I ought to know."

Trustingly, she looked up at me with her sightless eyes.

"He's not a *bad* fellow, Nana. Just tricksy. We will have to be smart Owls to stay ahead of him."

"You are right, as usual. Now back to bed with you. Here's your ginger water bottle"—a sac of deer leather—"and I tied a skein of greeny yellow onto the end of the brown yarn you are knitting. Here's your cedar whistle on a new thong"—putting it around her thin neck—"so you sing out if you want me to fetch you anything else."

The quakes continued for three more days. Winona, feeling much better, came to Circle the third day. When the baton was passed to her, she clambered to her feet and said, "Coyote danced himself into my dream. There was a goatskin with a lot of teensy writing on it. He knocked over the beer barrel and spilled the beer on the ground. It foamed like crazy. He put the goatskin over the beer jar and stretched it tight to make a big drum. Then he danced like a mad dog on top. The drum boomed and shook the trees. Spiky things fell out of the sky and hit me on the head and stuck all over my hair. I wasn't hurt. Coyote kept saying, 'I'm gonna shake things up, but *good*. Shake 'em up but *good*, oh yeah, yeah, yeah, yeah, yeehaw!'"

She sang out the last five words, to a Beatles tune and a Rebel Yell. She was an Oddfellow all right! I was proud of her for speaking up so plain and without the least awkward pause. Our practice sessions had taken root. Nobody laughed nor rolled their eyes at her dream. Not since she predicted the wildfires that overran Catalpa Clan's summer cow pasture. Instead, we all sat in silence after she sat down, wondering what the message might mean.

We barely felt the tremors here, but I wondered if the folks in what our youngsters call "Big White Swampumland"—the coastal midlands of old Virginia—would have had much building damage. Bad for the pipes, good for the guttersnipes. Guttersnipes being a slang word for teen gangs that paw through "ur-bubble rubble" to get at the copper and glass and whatnot. To do them justice, they do rescue people from fallen buildings in the worst crises. But they didn't always have such good manners and common sense. They had to be taught by fedders and hoodwatch snipers to be nice. And the Restorative Justice teams that filtered down this way from Vermont and up from Brazil did a lot to bring the Balance back into community life.

Well, I was right and I was wrong about the quakes and the river houses. Hey, fifty percent ain't so bad. Even Ty Cobb only batted .357, lifetime. We left our snugs, snow camps, and winter lodges round about the Ides of March. To celebrate, we ate a Caesar salad from the hoop house greens and poured Caesar dressing over it made with goat curds.

"I come not to praise Caesar but to eat him," I declaimed grandly. "Render unto Caesar that which is Caesar's"—pouring on the dressing—"and unto Odd, that which is Odd."

Myself, being the oldest and Oddest, I was duly crowned with the Silly Hat and we ate our salads in a reverent, crunchy silence. The goat curd dressing was superb—or rather, super-herbed.

I do love having rich relations among the Hill Chaps. Their herbal medicinals kept me and my sickly young'un alive. Their spice trade ships go to Africa and India, not just to South Carolina. Their angora wools kept us oldsters busy all winter, cranking away on the sock machine, in the warm, sunny weave rooms, singing rude women's songs among delighted, shocked girls and disapproving, tongue-clucking, blanket-weaving mothers.

And, not to be despised, their sheepskin seconds, not good enough for trade but *quite* good enough for charitable giving to an old granny, kept our legs dry and our feet toasty warm on the muddy chilly tramp down to the Black Bottoms—what used to be pig farming country, and still had bad patches of chemical residue all over.

But we were smart, us Owly folk. We had planted tulip poplars that cleared heavy metals and fecal coliform out of the soil for *years* before we sold the lumber and redressed the topsoil with our homemade compost. Oh, that was a glory day, when the trees came down and made a lovely balance in our clan's Resource Book. My share was quite large, being proportional to the hours in my Time bank. If I die before it is exhausted, I got a dispensary order to transfer the remainder to Winona. She might have a lover some day or wish to adopt a child. A little bit of cash would be a good start for them.

The trees fell down and the lumber floated up—transported on the big Alco-aluminum canal barges that lock up and down between here and the Black Rock mills. And the smelly loads of manure and compost came down too, the next day, by coal train. What a grand gala it had been! We hired hands from here to Cahokia, as my folks used to say, and there was a pig slaughter held in the next county and what food, fun and frolic we had. I misremember how many Owl clan babies were born in late July the year after the Poplar Harvest—but it was quite a few. We even had a new fiddle tune named after us. Some scrawny old mountain man took a shine to us (or someone took moonshine to him) and made us into a tune: Owl Clan Dancing in the Poplar Grove. I hear it now and again when the Shakori bards come through. Winona put words to it, different words every time, always rude. She makes me laugh.

The quakes didn't harm the river bottom houses at all. Like I thought. The spring rains, however, did a *hell* of a lot of damage. The ones that were not piling-sprung got so moldy that you could not stay in them overnight. Well, it was way too wet to plant, so, sighing, we dismantled the summer sheds, took down canvas, clapboard panel sides, the gauze screened, nicely louvered frame-built vent-windows and hauled all, piece by piece, piling by piling, into the Potters' barn to dry out in the hot air piped from the kilns.

Warned by my February bad feeling, I had gone ahead and rented space in the Dry Barn just in case. Good thing. We were not the only clan affected, but we earned our name for smarts by being first to pull out of a bad year. We camped on higher-dryers, and fished a lot throughout April. There was nothing else to do.

We had no experience in rice farming, like our indigo-and-rice trading partners in Charleston, nor had we any seed rice to plant. We went ahead with our experimental mound-and-ditch culleys, though. Only in these culley-valley Hi-Lows did the crops prosper—everywhere else was too soggy for flakes. The corn stooked, and the barley foundered; had sukebind sprung up we would not have been surprised. Nor had we a hoot piece to flitch it with. Cold Comfort Farm is what we called ourselves, laughing ruefully.

In late spring, the sun came out—and stayed there. All the rain we could have used was used up already, I guess. Even the Hi-Lows had trouble with steady, relentless, unwavering sunshine. The squash grew too fast and the corn not fast enough. The beans did okay but nothing special and we were rather low on beans in the surplus stores.

Argh. I hate global weirding. No, not hate, it's just—it throws me off balance. Dammit, I am *old*, and I am *tired* of dealing with all these changes. Well, I could not complain. Compared to our next field neighbors, we were doing all right. We had fished up a storm and dried all our take before the horrid wave of pfisteria came up river. People were starting to look a little queer in our direction, so I thought maybe we had better pay a visit to some of our relations.

We left a gift of dried fish for the Potters, in addition to a full month's rent, though we left ten days early. It never hurts to leave people a little in your debt. Not a lot, mind you. Just enough to tip the balance uswise. The Hill Chaps were delighted with our fishy presence and presents, and not too perturbed by prognostications of a bad year for beer. They had worked a deal with the wine growers two years ago that was just now beginning to bring maplewood barrels down from the hills filled with sour apple ciders and wild muscadine wines. Oak was in short supply; Kentuckians got most of it for their whiskies.

It was hoped that the maple barrels would temper the sour wines and vice versa. Without the cost of charring.

"We'll soon find out, won't we?"

"Any day now, I expect. We'll send you the second samples, Cousin Anna. The first we're keeping for ourselves."

"Good," I said. "If it's *really* bad, you'll drop dead first, and *I'll* inherit the farms." They laughed.

In May we planted our summer gardens around the buildings of Winterhome. We oldsters and kidlets stayed put. We tend to the weeding while the young folk tend to their breeding. Just a joke. They do their mating pretty much in May then get down to work in the fields. Not much energy for flirty-sports down to the Bottoms. At least not most years. This year, who knows? Maybe a roll in the stunted hay was all that could be salvaged from an ill-distributed, damned, droughty, stock-broke sort of year. I heard that we rebuilt our river cabins on a stretch of higher ground, but that was about all she wrote.

Come September, we knew it was going to be a dead loss of a year for harvest. We were not *worried* exactly. We knew our surplus stores would see us, if dully, through the winter. Our kinfolk and other relations were generous and would invite us around to give us some variety. We could count on good greens from the hoop houses even in February, some years.

There would be deer meat and wild duck, and my land, Canada goose needed to be thinned if the slime on the roads was any indication. It was not the loss of one harvest that made us feel so dispirited. It was—I have to admit it—it was the loss of prestige. We like to be two steps ahead of the rest of the world. No question but we would have to dance backward this year. Our much vaunted Hi-Lows were not exactly a wash-out. But they were not exactly a trumpet-sounding triumph either. Oh, well. I suppose there are just some years when Coyote pisses into the beer.

And then the hurricanes came.

Winona hobbled into my Elder's longhouse, all a-tremble and seeking me. I was already awake and stirring, so I met her a few steps from the doorway. She did not venture beyond the Spirit Line, for all her fear. What a good girl she always was!

"Yes, my dear," I said, "tell Lee-Lee to fetch your ponies. You'll have to warn them."

She could not hobble fast enough, so she hopped onto her specially made scooter and zoomed off. I went round to the stables to get a bike helmet small enough to fit each of the girls. Lee-Lee, as lazy a lump as ever mocked a clod of red clay was, for a wonder, alive and awake today. She caught the ponies in record time and had them saddled by the time I came back with road food, a medicine pak each for horse and riders, a solar water distilling kit, and two leather bottles of much watered green apple wine.

"Here are the red flags," I said, handing them each a yard-long bamboo pole bearing the traditional signal: two flags of red with black squares in the center. "Stay together till you get to Mudball Camp. Then split up. But not till then. Lee-Lee, you know the way south, warn the Dockers. They may already know what's coming, but warn them anyway. Winona, child, you rest at Mudcamp before you go any farther. It's a long way, honey, and your pony will be tired. Don't let the ponies eat too much trash. Borrow hay from folks along the way if they are willing. When Lee-Lee gets back from the Dockers, go together to warn the rest of the folks. There's time, don't fret and don't push the ponies harder than they want to go."

It was a ripping storm. I mean that in every way you think. In the floodplains, especially. What it didn't rip, it tore. The news came back to us oldsters in slowly assembled bits, as first one courier then another returned. The flag signal outposts were restored after a day or two, and then news came in faster. It was a week before most of the downed and damaged radio nets were fully operational.

News for Owl Clan was mostly bad. Our river houses were blown apart and the pieces scattered inland. Every field, even the Hi-Lows had been inundated with salt waters. And Winona, instead of waiting at Mudball Flats, as expected, had apparently gone mad.

"I have to find them," she said, and rode off on her pony after only an hour's wait.

"We did not know what she meant to do until it was too late."

"We were portaging the boats up to the Potters' fields and she was gone before we knew it."

"Don't worry, though. Eduardo will find her. He knows that whole Table from Swamp to Notch. He'll find her."

"More likely she'll lose them both! All the channels will be changed now, the Dockers said so. She disobeyed you Nana Anna! If she dies it's her own fault!" Lee-Lee burst into tears, afraid she was going to be blamed.

I shook my head. "No need to panic and cast blame, my dear. We're all tired and dirty enough without slinging soul mud about. As for Winona, if she disregarded my instruction there must have been good reason. She's not lame in the head, only in limb. And she's not an under-seven anymore. It's not me or you or anyone she answers to now. She has to obey her Guides," I said. Outwardly calm, yes, but like I always say, I do not tell all I know, nor mention to just anyone when I notice a leaden weight taking the place of my heart.

Days went by. I tended the garden. I remembered all I could about the dream of Coyote dancing on the goatskin drum with tiny writing. I waited to hear the worst of the news.

But she came back! She and Eduardo came back, perfectly sound of mind and wind, with seven thin brown strangers and a strange-looking burden bound up in waterproofs and blankets on the pony's back. I summed the strangers up in a glance: a fine set of sailors—but Cape Fear got its name for a reason.

Winona was beaming.

"We FOUND em, Nana!" she said, and flung herself into my arms.

I looked over her head at our guests and said, "Forgive me if I greet the little one before you. She is a special child."

"I'll say she is," said the ship's captain. "And I wish we had one like her. Wouldn't be here without her."

"And Eduardo," Winona amended.

"Him too. Ver' glad to have the pleasure of making your acquaintance, Ma'am."

"Welcome all to Owl Clan's hearthstone."

I dipped from our well and drank and gave them also to drink from the dipper.

"We will meet to join in a thanks meal in about an hour. Winona, please take your sister-guests to the bath pool and show them their sleeping and eating lodges. Eduardo will attend to you, brothers. Lee-Lee, I hope you will help your sisterkin by looking after her pony. You see no harm has come to her, and we are all most thankful."

Lee-Lee did as she was bid without any backchat. This incident seemed to have woken her up. She was the better forever for having had a serious fright at the age of nine. Maybe she had a latent touch of warrior blood in her.

The field harvest was not the worst of the losses we sustained. Our new poplar and cypress plantations were tore up. We made the best of it by taking the downed trees to make a pair of shore-going vessels as a magnificent gift to the Wikifen. The young men were wildly enthusiastic as they carved, hewed, burned and carpentered up a matched set of three-beam "castaway canoes" or compound outriggers, stabilized for moving in coastal waters by retractable keel plates at each end.

Drawn up and cantilevered back, the end keels do not hinder the triple hulled canoes from nosing about in the shallows. They can even slide across high reefs. Lowered, the fore and aft keel plates stabilize the outrigger formation for riding deeper ocean waves. We also supplied them with one of our custom made, time- and river-tested sampan sails. We used the salvaged riverhouse canvas for the sail. The bamboo battens are stuffed with lightweight rods of recovered plastic (for extra flex) and wrapped with polyester thread-cord to lessen the risk of cracking and splintering, plus making the battens smooth as silk to handle. No one yet has duplicated our secret formula glue.

On the Outer Banks they call these craft "rigamarrees." That's a Port Manteo word-cross between rigamarole and outrigger, with the Mare Seas thrown in for good measure. The Wikifen planned to tow the rigamarrees until they learned how to sail them, but the Pod People at New Bern were happy to loan them the Wilson twins for a voyage north. A nice *long* voyage.

Bad news continued to come in. Our denim partners' indigo fields were ruined. We surprised them by placing an order for lots of undyed cloth to replace our river cabins. We think we will try a yurt superstructure, on a houseboat base instead of cabins on pilings. The yurt walls could be made from splintered remains of our old cabins. Now to come up with some kind of cross ventilation that works in muggy weather. Yurts are fine for winter, but awful stuffy in summer. Can't roll up the sides at night, not where the big Bottomland eato-skitoes whine.

Then I had the Big Idea of the Great Reed Gathering. We could send our young folk down to Charleston to help with a harvest of all the raw fibers that the storms blew down. We could all go, if there was food enough. Nettles, river canes, everything we could reach without leech. The losses in one field could mean abundance elsewhere. We could harvest fibers till our scalps stung.

Of course you have to be prudent and put away in a bumper year for a lean one. But we needed cheap, thin cloth—lots of it—and had no harvest to speak of. Why not let the beans and taters go to seed? Buy cloth with the work of our hands?

The more I thought about it, the better the idea looked. A rope-making festival. Downed poplars for mini masts. Harvest the hemp and jute windfalls. A linenfest. The flaxseed crop could be pre-retted in place, right there in Nature's Big Salty Vat. Beg, borrow, or (last resort) hire a coal-steam baler and a twiner's rig and crew. Trade the bales upriver to the mills for mountain produce that escaped the storms—could be done, could be done, yes. Tricky, but could be done.

But first, had to see to the guest duty. Meant I would have to go to Black Rock though. Negotiations. On foot. Horses all in use for rescue and cleanup work. No help for it. Start now. Ugh. Long way for old bones and young cripples. But it was better than moping around, gazing at downed plantations and ruined fields.

Well, we did not have to walk all the way, after all. The Hill Chaps gave us a berth halfway on their wine run. Then we hitched a ride on a hay wagon for a couple of hours. We missed the slow-go compost and manure train that loops out of town into the country all day and all night long. We would have waited till the next one came round, but a fellow with a load of new potatoes was taking a hand pump cart along the narrow-gauge rail lines into town. He was glad to have me and Eduardo to spell him on the pump, so even with our extra weight, he got to town quicker and less tired too.

We had a meal at my third cousin's-second-marriage-son's-in-law's house and told them all the news, or at least the parts of it that suited our purposes. Then we washed our faces and hands, put on our finest come-to-trade tablet-woven silk baldrics pinned with all our best insignia, and made our way on foot to Miller's Row.

I had not been here for a long time. I had sent messages to the Justice Circles now and then, and of course, we kept up with the Court news and the County Water Reports. Eduardo would have to drop off his post-hurricane channel sketches and ask for a cartographer to visit the Banks as soon as the snows permitted.

I had not been here in a long time, but I knew a lot about this town. I knew where we would have to go to get the best deal.

It would have to be a big miller's place and the biggest, baddest, geariest miller of all: Big Arn. Yep. Nothing would do but the very best. Arnold's Gear Reclamation and Design. That's what the sign says, and has done for lo these fifty years.

"We have a shipwrecked crew down our way, Arn," I said, "and they need a new sextant. Theirs went overboard, worse luck. Lost a good man too."

He didn't answer right away,

"What's in it for us?" *In* a surly tone, if you please, and even if you don't. "We don't work for free, you know. You gonna fee 'em?"

"Depends on the fee structure," said I.

"Hmmph. 'Nother one of your stray kids and bleating ewe lambs?"

"W-e-l-l," I said, drawling out my words like an old, wit-wandering, lecture-licking woman, "if they was kids and lambs you could feed 'em up and get parchment and vellum, not to mention lamb saag and good goat jerk for winter's feast. But as it happens they ain't neither one."

He paid me no mind, just went on a-measuring and making tick marks on a cypress wooden gear blank with a fat pencil. He didn't impress me. I knew he was making a replacement gear for the Johnson County windmill that got wrenched about when a line broke and two of the vanes unreefed themselves and bellied out full in the storm. Those cheeseparing JoCo millers—they saved the cost of a bale or two of our good cord and had to pay instead for a brand new gear. Sarve 'em right. But I didn't say anything about it. I know more than I say and say less than I mean. Usually.

"As it happens," I said, "They are the Wikiexpedia Team out of Tampa and they lost their scout in the storm."

Well! His head came up like a borderdog scenting smoke. A fire of greed, cunning and deep hunger to learn, learn, learn blazed out of his unshielded eyes. He was always easy to read, if not to control. But I had him by the brass cojos this year.

"*And* they're under Owl Clan's protection *and* intercoastal waterway salvage law applies. So if anything, ah, *unfortunate* should happen to them or their cargo, I would certainly have to talk to your sister about it."

Arn's sister was the acting warchief for Brassball Clan—they had no older women left since the flu three years gone—and she was timid by nature, and indecisive. Besides, she was pregnant again and would be far more willing to make undignified concessions in Owl's favor to protect her unborn and make sure our midwives would be there for her in her time. We had an unbroken line of Triangle nurse-doctors and our midwives were second to none in the Neuse Shed and Lumbee Nations.

What's more, she and I both knew who had set wild dogs on to harry our sheep and killed Winona's mother seven, no eight, eight and a half years ago. Eight years, as Jane Austen says, can seem little more than nothing.

Some people call me Wild Dog Killer or Oakly-Moakly Annie, or Miss Domination, or Batgirl or The Rifleman. Others just call me King Bitch. But not where I can hear them. I may be old but I still have my hearing. And I have other ways of knowing things. So does Winona. When there is need, the Knowing comes. Sometimes too early. Sometimes too late. But it surely comes.

"Got any use for a Wikipedia update, Arn?" Eduardo asked ever-so-casually. Arn breathed stertorously, carving his big gear, and did not answer.

"We might get one," Eduardo went on to inform him, "but our server is small and we'll have to choose carefully. It is so hard to choose between this and that. Not that we really *need* a more recent update. Cordage and yarns don't change all that fast. Not like metallurgy. Our last update was what? About ten years ago, right Nana?"

"Eight," I said in a cool tone. "Around the time Winona here was born."

"Well, who needs a Wikipedia update when you have a little Winnieminni-etonkawonka in your midst?" Eduardo teased, messing up Winona's hair. She turned shy and slipped behind me, clinging to my deerskin trousers. Old women wear trousers like men because we no longer shed the moonwise blood. Like men, we old women are war-makers. We may not draw the bow nor cast the spear but we know where to place a bullet point. Not always on a business presentation.

"Please do not call her by her baby name," I admonished our scout. "Not in front of our neighboring chieftain. We are conducting serious business here, my son."

"No harm intended, Elder Anna. Please accept my apologies, Winona Little-Bear." Winona forgave him readily, her eyes shining with hero-worshipping love. But she did not come out from behind me the rest of the visit.

I will spare you the account of the negotiations. As Winona says about Coyote, the Brassballs are not *bad* men—just tricksy. Not so much in brass as in precision tooling and labor. The sextant was indeed a costly item—but they owed us *big* time. And they knew it.

Besides, the Wikifen were no pushovers. They had plenty of time to wait while we were building them a shore going craft and the Outer Banksters were repairing the damage to their main hull. Slowly a deal was worked out, trading a partial Wiki dump, mainly to do with new discoveries and processes in metals, in exchange for a new sextant.

Also the Navi'Gator showed an interest in receiving the new sky charts and weather data kept by Brassballs' weird bro-clan up in Boone (the Daniels). He vowed to see that the charts would be provisionally added to Wiki, pending the final decision of the fact check teams that go out in Spring.

I yawned. Every guy wants a piece of the glory. Better satellite charts than other ways of spending their time. I dropped out of the negotiations in the first round, as soon as I saw the Wikifen could take care of themselves. So. There I was, just idly eating a rare fresh September nectarine in brilliant, post-hurricane sunshine, when my top favorite first cousin on my mother's side came down the hill with a roan mare and a clan-gift of breathtaking value: chestnuts.

"Thought I'd find you here," he said. "Saw you in a dream."

The sacksful of seed sorts were left in the protective burr for transport, but the ones for eating had been shelled already by my thoughtful and exceptionally hard-handed relations.

"You can try it out down your way. Or farther south. Maybe plant some where the tallest poplars went down in the storm. We are not sure if it will take in the warmer climate. But we think it will do well in the north country. It likes a little cold."

The Wikifolken received this precious commission with a little touch of awe. A cache of jewels was nothing to this. If the trees took root in Senecaland, if they were the ones to restore chestnut trees to the north country, their names would be remembered by Tellers for centuries—not just in Wiki, but in the traditions of every clan from the old Carolinas to old Canada. The storm clouds would have proved to have a silver lining indeed! And their fallen scout—he would be long remembered too.

Our own fallen had best be forgotten. For the sake of decency. Stupid, deadly, useless blundering malice has no part in a hero's tale. Let Coyote play that role. Best to keep the minds of children and young men elevated above the petty spites and revenges one people can inflict upon another. No, the whole truth would have to be hidden—passed down for a while among women. A warchief's secret knowledge that draws the deepest lines to her face, and constrains her judgment, and adds, ever so subtly, to her power.

And when, eventually, even that was forgotten—as so many evil deeds have been forgotten—why, so much the better for all our relations. A war chief has a duty to keep the peace for more than one generation. And, should there be a future need, then the Knowing was there—would always be there.

I had a brief vision—just a flash, really—of a land covered in tall chestnut trees, from New Bern to North Bering. Trees, trees, trees—an ocean of waving green branches.

It happened so fast. I can't be sure if it was a vision of the future or an intuition of the past. But there was a faint, faint whiff in the green-scented air of lasting prestige.

A little brown bear in the berry patch up the hill looked directly at me. I nodded. Perhaps, in the children's Tale of the Newy Chewy Chestnuts it would be a little bear that led my cousin down the mountain. Yes. That would be a more fitting memorial. A Great Horned landed on a branch near me. We looked at one another. She flew off into the dusk, alone, a field mouse in one talon to feed her nestling.

‡‡‡

"I can scout for them," Eduardo said.

"No," I decided, even before Winona turned to me with teary eyes begging me not to let him go. "No, the northern branches of the Shore Clan are not to be trusted. Young male, good looking like you—sure, they'll kill you if they get the least chance. Same at New Haven. No, son. I'll have to send Sheila. They won't kill a mother with a newborn. Not even Yayalies are that savage."

"Sheila is not as good a scout as I am. I can keep myself out of trouble."

"No, brother," I said, promoting him from son to brother on the spot, "I need you here. I have a mission for you that no other can complete." I whispered to him my plan to steal the technique of galvanizing steel from Brassball clan. We might wrangle some tin powder out of the Hill Chaps after their next voyage to Wales. If we did manage to grow chestnuts I wanted to have a stock of galvanized steel buckets to collect them in the fall.

And to tap sugar maples in late winter. I was tired of running out of honey in February. I make long range plans, whether they ever get carried out or not. Can't help it.

Aloud I said, "Sheila may not be as good as you—few are. But she is your sister-kin and she has a child now. That will sharpen her skills. She'll learn. And she can teach you when she gets back. Your turn will come, brother. Patience is a scout's best quality. You see, Winona agrees with me. I am not just being a dull, overcautious old woman."

"'Fraid she's right, nevvie. I brought the seed down from the mountains, so now a woman has to carry the seed up the coast. It keeps the Balance. If we send another male as the Guardian, the Spirits might take it as impiety and disregard." Reluctant and not convinced, but submissive to an Elder's decision, Eduardo nodded sadly.

"Cheer up, bro," said one of the Wikifen, tapping his channel book, "Your name's on this chart already. We aren't likely to forget seeing your ugly face come out of that swamp with anti-venom in hand."

"And if you rechart the new channels for our return trip," said the ArchiMede, grinning, "we'll bring you back some hot porno from Old Manhattan."

Eduardo turned bright red and could not speak for embarrassment. "Or some Jersey horse opium!" enthused the 'Gator.

Both young men felt the sharp prick of my gimlet eye and the expedition leader quickly said, "Just kidding, ma'am. But we really do need the map of the new channels. Trade for what you want, honest."

Eduardo suddenly found his tongue. "Can you bring us some phonograph needles?"

"Mebbe so. What model, bro?"

The Wikifen went off with Eduardo eagerly leading the way to inspect our ancient, brass-spring wind-up record player. Winona loved listening to Beethoven and Mahler and Telemann. She said the music helped her to really see.

I made sure a spare spring of new brass was included in our share of the salvage bounty. Why! The scraps from cutting the sheet for the sextant would do wonderfully well! I said, innocently ignorant. They got the point, and I got the spare spring. If any hot porno changed hands between the Fen and the Brass after formal negotiations were concluded, at least they had the decency to do it out of my line of sight.

The rest of our Cirkin stood around chattering like a flock of jays. My cousin and I quietly gloated over the chestnuts, about the potential for riches if the strain took hold: wood, food, shelter, game—*whew*.

"It's a blight resistant half breed between the Asian and the native American strains."

"Like us." I grinned.

The young people of Black Rock looked at us: shocked, scandalized. Racetalk!

We laughed. Owl clan is famous for making jokes in poor taste.

REVIEWS

The Great Bay:
Chronicles of the Collapse
by Dale Pendell

North Atlantic Books, 2010

THIS NOVEL TAKES A PANOPTIC view of the San Francisco Bay area over increasing increments of time, starting in the early 21st century and ending sixteen thousand years in the future. It is a story of rising sea levels and the string of cultures which emerge from the dissolution of industrial civilization. As with any good story the marks and scars of transformation are what make the protagonist stand out. In this case that character just happens to be the California bioregion and the main event is the rising level of the Bay as climate change and melting ice sheets do their inimitable work.

The book is structured at first in increments of decades, then a half-century, moving on to centuries, and finally millennia, all in the space of 275 pages. I consider the book a condensed lesson in future history. At the beginning of each section is an overarching summary of changes in the world climate, water levels and significant happenings among humans and animals. Gradually the San Francisco Bay turns into the Great Bay, spreading inland and as far north as Feather River and on down to the southern reaches near the San Joaquin River. Dale includes a number of different maps in the text, adding a touch of topographical realism to the work.

After the scenery is taken in as whole the author zooms in to look at slices from the lives of a number of different humans, the communities they live in, and how they cope with the world around them. This is done through straight narrative but he also provides excerpts from newspaper reports, diary entries, and interviews as collected from the archives of a fictional Scholars Guild, and later from the Colleagues of Thermocene Studies. This approach creates the feel of a compilation, and shows how variable human cultures can be, how much they change over time, and how future dwellers of this planet might interpret the remnants of our own.

In the first couple of decades after collapse he deals with themes of rampant disease, martial law followed by anarchy, and the disintegration of infrastructure. After this widespread chaos, individuals joined together in bands and tribes, driven by necessity and happenstance. The first mini tale in the book is that of Amanda, ordered out of her house by her dying mother. Meeting up with a girl named Inez they escape the plague and litter of dead bodies in L.A. and head up the coast, eventually falling in with a group of bikers known as the Roadkill Rangers. Inez is later interviewed in the book. In the second century section a story is told about Ranger Fly, one of the kids who grew up in the Kern Roadkill Collective, a community that evolved from the bikers. Fly left this group to forge a path in the wilderness, spending a lot of solitary time in the mountains. He eventually decided to become one of the trained trackers tasked with watching and guarding the region for the Confederation and their militias. His story weaves in bits of history about the little and big invasions, skirmishes and wars.

In one of the longer episodes Solomon the Monk travels from the Bay to Boulder, Colorado to celebrate the second centennial of the collapse on the 4th of July. Over the course of the three month trek they must evade slavers, cannibals and petty barons, only to get captured by barbarians after all.

Yet life is not all conflict. Mechanics, poets, herbalist beer brewers and electricians also populate the land around the Great Bay. Guilds specializing in passing on diverse skills and trades proliferate. People go out in their boats and look at the remains of San Francisco underneath the waves as they fish.

As time progresses the cultures described in the book begin to look like foreign countries. Barriers of language begin to emerge. Continuity is fragmented. Poets are once again keepers of memory, and some take the task of memorizing bits of Samuel Taylor Coleridge, and other poets who may now already seem old to us. These old poems are in "Precle," the language I am writing in, and most people outside of the poets barely understand it anymore.

As the book proceeds further into the deep time of the future the stories take on mythopoetic qualities, as if they could have been drawn from our own deep past and archaeological records. Dale Pendell makes for a grand sweep of a number of the different trajectories the collective future could go, taking in to account the loss of cheap sources of renewable energy and the limits imposed by an ecosystem that has been altered by climate change. What remains constant in each era he explores is the essential relationship between people and place. From the disruptions caused by a sprawling technoculture and in its gradual disappearance, humanity returns to an awareness that engagement with nature is both visceral and harmonious.

- Justin Patrick Moore
sothismedia.com

The Well
by Catherine Chanter

Atria Books, 2015

The Water Knife
by Paolo Bacigalupi

Alfred A. Knopf, 2015

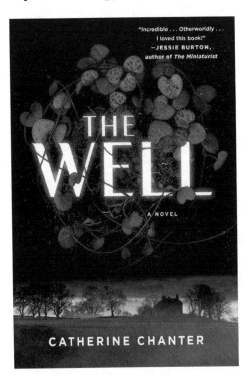

"Incredible... Otherworldly...
I loved this book!"
—JESSIE BURTON,
author of *The Miniaturist*

THE WELL

A NOVEL

CATHERINE CHANTER

THERE ARE MULTIPLE WAYS OF tackling our deindustrial future in narrative form. Paolo Bacigalupi's *The Water Knife* and Catherine Chanter's *The Well* exhibit two of them. The former studies it as harsh reality, exposing an American Southwest dying from need of a drink, dusted with human cruelty and exploitation, and flaunting the frayed edges of survival. The latter brings a touch of magical realism to the English countryside, turning the thirsty consequences of climate change into a mystery, sprinkling it with the vaguest backdrop of social unrest, and burrowing into the psyche of its lead character.

The Well takes a myopic view of the future and turns it into an intensely personal, poetic and wandering exploration of one woman's life: her failing marriage, strained relationship with her daughter, dead grandson, slow absorption into a cult, and her very sanity. In this novel, set in an undetermined point in the near future, the consequences of our destructive ways of living are used as stage setting and occasional plot driver, rather than as an important reality to be explored in and of itself. Britain is seized by a devastating drought and its disruptive effects echo across the countryside, creating political and economic turmoil and leading to an increasing agitation and unpredictability amongst the populace. Ruth Ardingly, the novel's protagonist, and her husband Mark watch this disruption play out in her home country from the awkward position of her family's country estate, nicknamed "The Well," where it regularly rains under the cover of night.

Unsurprisingly, this is both a blessing and a curse. Ruth's farmer neighbors grow ever more suspicious and angry as their fields brown and die while The Well remains lush, green, and bountiful. They suggest water thievery; some malicious maneuvering around the drought-imposed restrictions. As the drought drags on and the population becomes more and more desperate, the existence of The Well and its damp, green pastures begins to draw not only scorn and anger, but tresspasses, pilgrimages, and a religious cult's fervor. Against the backdrop of this rising tension, Chanter layers in family and interpersonal drama, weaving Ruth's daughter and grandson into the haunting and tragic narrative that echoes from the book's opening pages and is painstakingly revealed through the novel's looping time shifts.

Chanter's language is consistently beautiful, her prose poetic, and the story features a multitude of conflicting elements that, on paper, should weave into a compelling tapestry. And yet, *painstaking* is no accidental choice in describing the plot's unfolding. Chanter too often opts for poetry over plot movement and a novel that clocks in at just under 400 pages feels far too long. Chanter does an excellent job of plunging Ruth into the category of unreliable narrator and making the reader suspect her motives and actions, yet it eventually reaches the point where we just want to know what the hell is going on rather than working through another ten pages of impressive linguistic manipulations that have grown stale in their lack of clarity.

Eventually Chanter does find her way to the story's denouement, slotting her many pieces into a relatively satisfying conclusion. However, here again we come to the ways in which decline is treated in fiction and Chanter's resolution of the broader collapse themes—the drought and resultant unrest—are too easy. Yet she can't be faulted. This, ultimately, is not a novel dealing with climate change and social unrest; it's a deep dive into one woman's troubled mind and the spiraling chaos both within and around her. The resolution is fine within that context, though it tells us little about the likely futures we face.

IN BACIGALUPI'S THE WATER KNIFE, on the other hand, reality is harsh, often brutal, and assiduously avoidant of simple resolutions. This vision of the future is a dramatically different one than Chanter's. There are no rain-kissed pastures; only vast, dry, and dusty deserts. There are no comfortable English countryside lifestyles; mostly just painful lives lived within the ruins of the American Southwest. Humanity is tangled deep in the chaotic covers of its (un)made bed and, while Bacigalupi litters the landscape with compelling characters for us to root for and against, his primary goal seems to be to unearth an unsettling vision of the world we're making for ourselves.

Water has all but disappeared in the American West and Southwest in *The Water Knife*, with irrigation systems proving no match for the resultant thirst of so many millions living in drylands never meant to support such populations. Economic, political, and legal battles have broken out among California, Arizona, and Nevada, and the strength of the federal government is crumbling in the face of states fighting for their very survival. Against these political and ecological realities, Bacigalupi sketches out economic, class, and ethnic divisions that will feel unnervingly familiar to readers. While Phoenix is dying, Las Vegas thrives—not due to natural advantages, but to the successful wielding of wealth and power by Catherine Case, the putative ruler of the Nevada desert. Using the main character, Angel Velasquez, as her power broker who deals in activities both legal and illegal, she brings to bear a cunning cruelty that allows her

to divert the waters of the Colorado River to her massive arcology developments, which serve as a combination of home, respite, and playground for those rich enough to buy their way into them.

The legal basis for these diversions, though, comes under question with rumor of a major water rights find in Phoenix—a document capable of rewriting the rules. Case dispatches Angel to Phoenix to follow the trail and head off any trouble before it can reach the court system, and the story takes off from there. Lucy Monroe enters as a young journalist carved sharp by the jagged realities of a collapsing Phoenix and begins a long dance with Angel as he attempts to make sense of the rumor and reality.

As he lays out his world for us, Bacigalupi exhibits an impressive ability to tease present trends and realities out into a dystopian near-future that feels all too possible. While some might legitimately quibble with the feasibility of massive arcologies, it seems just enough within the realm of possibility—given an economic and political landscape still able to concentrate enough wealth and resources to create these fragile and temporary outliers—to keep the story from becoming a victim of scifi techno tropes. Similarly, this future features Twitter, Teslas, and other relics of our current technology, but convincingly portrayed as the hangers-on of a dying reality. This is an all-too-recognizable future wracked by change and devastation, swiftly approaching its end date, which at least some of the characters welcome with open arms.

Indeed, one of the major themes of the novel is the question of expectations and acceptance, embodied by Maria Villarosa, a young Texas migrant trying to stay alive in the shredded underbelly of Phoenix. Her struggle highlights deep divisions between those who are willing to accept the harsh new reality of life in an ecologically devastated world, and those who are fighting the new reality. As the story rumbles on, her internal questions about whether or not to accept this new world at face value or to cast back to past expectations in the hope of a better future provide some of the story's weightier philosophical musings.

Bacigalupi crafts his world with care, clueing us in time and again to its realities without bogging the reader down in exposition and explanation. Clearsacs, for instance, show up early in the story and we have a basic understanding of their function via context long before the novel makes it explicit in later pages. The convoluted political landscape is laid out with a deft authorial hand, through a combination of conversation, action, and exposition that achieves its task without wandering too far abroad. Ethnic and class divisions are defined through scene and action, as well as through the crossing of state and regional boundaries by the central characters.

In the end, Bacigalupi does not mince words. He throws the future we're creating in our face, forcing us to look upon its misery, even as he brings us along in a flurry of plot and action, at a swift and gripping pace, with the constant dance of well-defined and sympathetic characters. Unlike Chanter, he offers no easy ecological outs in the novel's final pages, yet his conclusion is satisfying all the same. This tattered world continues to crumble, even as he avoids the trap of wallowing in nihilism. This is an honest future that Bacigalupi presents to us, and it's an example of the sort of narratives we need as we contemplate and accept the schism between what we collectively expect and what the world is in the process of serving us.

- Joel Caris

CODA

Writing the Future

by Joel Caris

It's impressive the degree to which we flatten the future. Do an image search online for the term "science fiction" and you'll find an endless stream of computer generated images of alien cities and landscapes. You'll find spaceships and rockets and alien lifeforms. Some of it will be dystopian, but even that usually consists of the same, aforementioned alien cities, just broken and crumbling rather than shiny and new. This is the science fiction future, it seems, always and forever: a string of *other places* borne out of the rictus narrative of unending progress. Placing it here on Earth—except when Earth has become unrecognizable—is practically verboten. We must go elsewhere. We must go to the stars. That is the only place we can find our future science.

I admit even I feel that way at times. Sifting through a pile of stories to find the five exemplary works published in this issue left me often feeling as though I wasn't looking for science fiction stories per se, but simply good stories. *Is this really science fiction?* I wondered. *Or are these just good stories set in the future?*

Well, they're both. And the simple truth of it is that these stories better represent the sort of hard realities the scientific method offers us than the vast majority of science fiction being published today. Why, for instance, are the agricultural methods and hand tools of *'Naut* and *Coyote Year*, the glider from *American Silver*, the ships in *The Last Knut of Linsey Island* or the loom upstairs in *The Specialist* lessor technologies than a spaceship travelling across interstellar space? They aren't. And unlike that spaceship, they all are technologies that can or do exist. They're far more science-based than the myth of humans hopping between planets at some undetermined point in the future, harnessing some magical source of unending power.

It's funny editing a science fiction magazine. It doesn't matter what your stated intent is or how specific your website is about the sort of work you're looking for, you're still going to get stories about mining asteroids, finding new sources of fuel even more powerful and fantastic than fossil fuels, and blowing away aliens. They've shown up in my inbox again and again. That, after all, is science fiction, and *Into the Ruins* is a science fiction magazine. *Ipso facto*, it must have stories set in space.

Except it doesn't. *Into the Ruins* exists to publish speculative fiction rooted in science. By that very definition, I will publish no stories of mining asteroids, of finding endless sources of energy, or of interstellar space travel by humans. Those are works of fantasy, not science fiction, because they are not rooted in scientific reality. But a small clan working the earth by hand hundreds of years from now? Now that's our future science.

So again, I put out the call. Let's stop flattening the future into space adventures that will never be. Let's instead widen and populate it with the millions of stories of humans right here on Earth that are actually rooted in scientific fact. Some of them will come across familiar, while others will strike us as more odd than any number of imagined civilizations strewn across the galaxy. But they are just as capable of fascinating and delighting us as any asteroid cowboys or insectoid aliens. Our planet is not boring or mundane. Let's spend some time exploring it and the futures it holds for us, shall we?

intotheruins.com/submissions

Questions? Comments? Email editor@intotheruins.com

Thank you for reading

Made in the USA
San Bernardino, CA
12 May 2016